OOPS, I'M DIVINE

Saving the World...by Accident

ISHANI KOMMERA

INDIA • SINGAPORE • MALAYSIA

ISBN
Paperback 979-8-89777-364-0
Hardcase 979-8-89984-625-0

CONTENTS

THE WORST LAST DAY OF SCHOOL

Every fairy tale starts with a 'once upon a time,' it has a charming prince, a beautiful princess, and an evil magic wielder who come together to a final battle face to face. Then it ends in a 'happily ever after.' This story consists of everything mentioned above, but there is no guarantee of a happily ever after. The princess is no 'Cinderella,' no 'Snow White,' no 'Rapunzel.' She is a normal teenager in the modern-world India who goes through what no one should ever go through. The unfortunate girl's name is Pooja.

Her story, like every story, did not begin with foreshadowing that something bad would happen. In fact, it started normally enough. Pooja woke up, went to school, and attended her classes like every weekday. Her school wasn't grand or gothic. It was a boring, five-story building, beige in color with a fine layer of dust, desperately in need of repainting. It stood tall and silent, giving no hints of the dangers lurking nearby. It was when the final bell rang, though, that her life turned upside down. When all the students filed out, happy chatter filled the air, signaling the end of the school year with the whole summer off.

Pooja and her two best friends, Thalia and Anaaya, were discussing their plans for hosting a party. While they were arguing about the party snacks, they accidentally bumped into their history teacher, Mrs. Mahi Singh. Her brown eyes glinted in humour as she turned around to face them, her scarf wrapped around her head to shield her from the heat, her silky hair up in a messy bun. With her pastel shirt and palazzo, she looked as stylish as ever.

"Oh my God, ma'am. I am so sorry, I didn't mean to bump into you," Thalia apologized, sounding sincere. Pooja bit back a laugh. Thalia acted like an angel sent from heaven in front of adults while she was anything but that. Mahi was the only one not fooled by any of her acts; this time was no exception either.

"That's completely all right, Thalia," she smirked, her brown eyes glinting in mischief. Maybe if you just stopped drooling over chocolate covered strawberries, this situation could have been avoided." This time, Pooja and Anaaya actually laughed. Their teacher knew their love for chocolate from the countless times they brought her baked goods loaded with it.

Suddenly, Pooja felt the sudden need to move out of the way. She grabbed Mahi's hand, pulled her into a crouch, and yelled, "Everyone, down! Now!" Not doubting her instincts, her friends fell to the floor. An arrow whizzed past her head and buried itself in the ground where Mahi was standing seconds ago. Feeling like cold metal was gripping her heart, Pooja cautiously got up and pulled the arrow out. There was a note tied to the base of the arrow which she carefully undid.

"I don't want to hurt anyone. I just want to talk to you, please give me one chance to explain myself. I should have done this years ago. Love, Prajwal," Pooja read out. "Anyone know any deranged people named Prajwal?" She meant it as a joke to lighten the mood, but the color fading from Mahi's face made her rethink her choice of words.

Mahi gently took the arrow from her hand and snapped it into two pieces because she was cool that way. Lips pursed, she took out her phone.

"I'm going to need you to leave, okay?" she ordered, sounding extremely tense.

"Ma'am, what happened?" Pooja asked. She did not like how her teacher was acting so out of the ordinary; sometimes she was uniquely unusual, but this time it was too much, the worry in her eyes too real.

"Nothing that concerns you unless you stay here for longer," she snapped.

"Umm… Poo? I think we should scram now, okay? Ma'am knows what she is doing, and let's not interfere," Anaaya suggested timidly.

Mahi turned back to her phone as though she had lost interest in the conversation. She dialed a number and waited three silent seconds before saying, "Hello Ahan? It is Prajwal, he is here in school. How fast can you come? 15 minutes? I… No, I am fine. I can manage, just make it quick, all right, there are three students with me right now. I told them to leave. No, I can't wait. That is…. Okay, you are right." She dropped the phone into the bag and turned to them. She looked like she had aged a few years in those seconds. "Look guys, trust me on this please. There is a dangerous guy I know, Prajwal, he is here. I need you to go home right now and pretend this never happened, okay?"

"Nobody is going home, unfortunately," a genuinely sad voice called out from straight ahead. They all turned quickly to see a man standing alone a few feet away.

He was a good height of around six foot three, wearing a floral shirt and shorts with fluorescent green Crocs. His hands were dug into the pockets, his thinning curly brown hair swaying due to the slight breeze. His milky brown eyes shone with victory while the rest of his face was pulled into a look of pity.

"Prajwal," Mahi uttered the word as if it carried a lot of weight.

"Mahi," he sighed, "Oh, it has been long, too long. How are you? How is Ahan?"

"Shut up, Prajwal. Stop it. You have no right to talk to me like that or to hold these kids here just because you couldn't get over the fact that I don't love you. I never did."

"Ouch, that hurt," Pooja thought, biting back a chuckle. She looked at her friends, expecting them to be laughing. Their terrified faces killed her urge to chuckle; maybe she should be taking this seriously, too.

"Oh, love, you really are brainwashed by darling Ahan," he chuckled. "You love him so much, do you not? Where is he now, when you need him the most? That's right, not here."

Pooja felt a strong urge to go up to Prajwal and punch his face. She did not know how Prajwal knew Mahi and Ahan, but Mahi talked a lot about their relationship, and Pooja knew it was beautiful and not at all toxic, as Prajwal was implying.

"Hey, Prajwal, right? Please don't think that all men treat women like you do. Some do love them and don't use them," she said sweetly.

"Your sass has only grown over the years," Prajwal chuckled.

Pooja was taken aback, 'Over the years?' As far as she knew, she had never seen this guy before, so why was he pretending like he knew her? She tucked that question in the back of her head to deal with later. Instead, she blurted, "I think you were dropped on your head when you were younger. I would remember if I met you before. Your face is unforgettable, it is *that* ugly. I suggest that you turn around and leave forever, for your own good. If she had it her way, Mahi ma'am could have killed you by now."

"What?" Prajwal smirked. "You have such great potential, dear. You should join me."

"That is only going to happen when I lose my mind, Prajwal," she rolled her eyes. This guy was giving her the heebie-jeebies, making her restless.

"You seriously don't remember the times when Ahan, Mahi, and I babysat you when you were two?"

"I don't know, genius. I was two, would I remember? I don't think so. Besides, Mahi ma'am never babysat me. I met her this year, as her student, and I don't even know Ahan that well!"

"What? It makes sense you would forget about me, but even..."

That was when all hell broke loose.

A man with an athletic body and amber-green eyes, filled with rage, slammed into Prajwal, sending him tumbling. His waves flew wildly around his face as he launched himself at him. His body moved with a fluid grace that showed the years of practice and hard work. Out of nowhere, a dozen heavily armed men jumped at him, pulling him away from the fallen Prajwal. Mahi yelled, "Ahan!" and ran to them, conjuring a spear wrapped in leather. She slashed and hacked as though she was born to do it. Together they kept the men busy. By then, Prajwal had recovered from the shock and was scooting away. Pooja noticed this and immediately decided he could not escape. He talked to her as though he knew her and she wanted some answers. She sprinted in his direction, jumping over the fallen bodies of men Mahi and Ahan knocked unconscious, and shoving him with all her strength, causing him to fall right back down.

"You are not going anywhere," she hissed, pushing her forearm against his throat. She then heard a cry of pain. She turned to see Thalia stabbed in the gut with an arrow. She was bleeding profusely and was on her knees with Anaaya trying desperately to stem the blood flow. Pooja turned, eyes wide with horror, to see who shot her friend. A muscular man in black was aiming another arrow at Thalia. Without thinking twice, she ran up to him and wrenched the bow out of his hands and snapped it in two pieces. She did not know where the strength was coming from, but it was there and it felt good. The man was staring down at her in shock. Even though he was at least a good six inches taller than her, she charged at him, punching him in the gut. She felt him deflate. Satisfied, she ran back to Thalia, who was lying on her back, a pool of blood surrounding her. Anaaya was trying her best to stem the blood flow, tears streaming from her eyes. Pooja looked to see Mahi and Ahan standing with their backs against each other, weapons drawn as the remaining men circled them.

Pooja's stomach churned. She felt the adrenaline pumping through her system, and she knew what she had to do. Leaving Anaaya to tend to Thalia, she walked toward the men, conserving her energy. She felt the desire to kill in every fibre of her body, a force of destruction begging to be set loose. She tapped into it, letting it take over her completely. She stalked around the men like a predator waiting for the kill and pounced on one, vaulting into the air and coming back down with full force. As she brought her hands down, she felt them close around a sword that perfectly fit into her grip and sliced him in half. Knowing that she would lose her nerve if she looked at the mutilated body, she turned away, joining her teacher and husband. Together, the three of them cut down each and every single man who dared to cross their paths. Pooja maneuvered the sword as if it were a part of her body, not realizing the amount of destruction she was causing with ease. Her body moved, but her brain didn't seem to be controlling it. It seemed to have shut down, letting muscle memory take over. That was absurd; she had never held a sword before, let alone fought with it.

Pooja looked at the blood that was splattered on the ground; her reflection stared back at her. But it was not the usual brown eyes and wavy black-haired girl staring at her; instead, it was the face of a warrior, the anger smouldering in her eyes and her face splattered with blood. The after-effects of the adrenaline rush seeped in, tiredness took over her whole being, and she sank to the floor, her head throbbing. She could hear nothing but her heart thumping against her ribs. She took a couple of breaths, calming herself down, and opened her eyes and stared at her hands, red with blood. 'The blood of the men you brutally murdered,' a voice inside her head whispered, 'You will be arrested, and you can kiss your dreams of Yale University goodbye.' Pooja shook her head and pounded the ground with her fists, releasing the rest of her anger.

Then, she realized that Anaaya was wailing her name. She quickly got up and rushed to her.

"What happened?" she snapped, her brain still not registering the events that had occurred.

"It's Thalia," sobbed Anaaya.

"What about her?" Pooja asked, glancing at her friend.

Her heart stopped. Her friend's face was deathly pale and eerily calm. Her shirt was completely soaked in blood, and she was as still as a statue. Pooja calmly walked up to her and grabbed her wrist. She waited, praying to all the gods that she did not believe existed, hoping that her friend was still alive. She sat there, motionless, trying to drown out the sobbing of Anaaya, desperate to hear a tiny little beat that would give her some hope that her friend could be saved. There was only silence.

No.

Pooja glanced up to see Anaaya holding Thalia's other hand, begging her to come back. She was trying to remind her of the fun times the trio had in hopes that Thalia would find her way back from the cold clutches of death. She was crying, showing her grief to the world without holding back. Pooja wondered why she wasn't. Why she could never express any emotions properly. Thalia used to be disappointed when she wasn't happy with the surprises she got from her friend. She *was* happy, she just didn't know how to show it. She would always try to explain, but to no avail. Thalia would be disappointed that Pooja wasn't mourning her death. Her *death*.

She could not believe the quirky, energetic Thalia Sharma was dead. She reached out and closed her empty, staring honey eyes. A warm tear trickled down her left eye and fell on her cheek. It was the first time she cried in years. An arm wrapped around her; it was familiar and comfortable. She buried her face in their chest, finding comfort in the slow stroking of her hair they were doing. She shuddered, glad for the comforting warmth enveloping her body.

"It's going to be okay," a voice soothingly whispered into her ear. She looked up to see Ahan holding her tight. She did not know why he was doing it, but it was helping, so she did not complain. She buried her face back into his chest and closed her eyes. She felt like time was ticking slowly. The pain of losing her friend never subsided, but her brain allowed more space for emotions. Her legs began cramping up really badly, so she pushed herself up.

"Thank you," she mumbled, surprised at how hoarse her voice sounded.

Ahan looked at her and smiled a genuine smile. "We are here to help each other, Pooja," he stood up, "Besides, I cannot thank you enough for helping us. If not for you, my wife and I would not have made it."

Pooja could only nod her head. She pulled Anaaya to her feet and said, "We have to tell her parents or call an ambulance."

"Unfortunately, we cannot do any of those things, Anaaya. It's about time we leave," Mahi sighed.

"Ma'am, with all due respect, may I remind you that Thals was our best friend for years? She has been there for us; now is the time she needs us most and you want us to leave?" fumed Anaaya, her voice cracking from the tears she held back. Pooja found a surge of anger breaking through her numb heart and clung to it. She couldn't believe how insensitive Mahi was being.

"Prajwal will be back," Mahi started.

"I don't care about him, alright? I just want my friend back. Now that I cannot have that, at least I want her to have a proper funeral!" Anaaya's strong attempts failed as tears ran down her face.

"Of course, you do," Ahan interrupted. "You can call Thalia's parents using the school telephone, call the police as well as your parents, Anaaya."

"What about me?" Pooja asked.

Ahan and Mahi looked at each other. Ahan's eyes softened, and he tilted his head as if to chide his wife softly. Mahi took a deep breath and held Pooja's hands.

"Pooja, Prajwal said some disturbing things about how we are related. He could be senile for all we know, but we cannot just brush away the fact that it could be true. We don't know how, but he knows you and we cannot risk him attacking you again. You must come with us to our base; there we can confirm and give you an all-clear."

"Okay," Pooja agreed hastily. She did not understand half of Mahi's words, but she wanted answers all the same.

She would think it through later, if she regretted it; she could always run away. She was no stranger to running away from her problems anyway. Ahan sighed and took out a bottle of clear liquid; he held it out to Anaaya.

"Drink this, please," he requested.

"Why?" she demanded.

"You obviously cannot roam around knowing that your best friend can do magic. It will drive you insane. This is a potion that will make you forget all the supernatural encounters you just had."

'Supernatural encounters? Like what?' Pooja asked. For all she knew, she had just murdered a couple of people for killing her friend and would be facing a few years in juvie. 'Murdered how?' a voice whispered in her head. She looked down at the floor, noticing the sword glistening in blood for the first time. The weapon that gave her the strength and courage to avenge her dear friend. However, she could not remember how she acquired it. Brows furrowed, she glanced at Ahan and Mahi for an answer.

Mahi reached forward as if to hold her hand, but thought better of it and said, "The ring that you always wear on your finger, you said your grandfather forced you to wear it. Now look at it."

She looked at the index finger of her right hand, but there was no ring to be seen. Immediately, she understood, "The sword is the ring!" she exclaimed in disbelief. Her grandfather knew she might need it. He was a psychic; he could see the future, as he claimed. Astrology. Pooja thought he was scamming people in his retirement, but now she couldn't be so sure about that. That meant her parents must've known; they must have powers too. Maybe her dad's power was being emotionally unavailable.

Anaaya stumbled toward her, "Pooja, this is crazy. I cannot deal with this. I am going to drink from that vial. I know I cannot support you any longer. I feel so useless right now, but I just cannot stand it, I..."

Pooja broke her off with a hug, which she did not do often. "Trust me, I love you. I don't want you to over-exercise yourself for me. Be safe. I don't think I will make it to Thals' funeral, just say that I am sorry to her parents. It is for the best," she mumbled into her ear. She had a sinking feeling that this would be the last time she would ever be this close to her friend because friendships can't work if you keep secrets from each other. It hurt, but she could not do anything about it. She would come back and work on her friendship with Anaaya later, once she figured out her and her family's involvement in whatever just happened.

"After you drink this, you will fall unconscious for a while. When you regain your consciousness, you will not remember much, just the bare minimum to make it look like a terrorist act," Ahan stated in a monotonous voice, making Pooja wonder how many times he had done this before and why.

Anaaya gave Pooja one last hug and downed the bottle in one go. Immediately, she fainted in Pooja's arms. She slowly laid her friend down next to Thalia, taking one good look at them before turning away.

Broken-hearted, she turned to Ahan, "Now what?"

Ahan took out an electric tablet from his backpack and opened it. Pooja discreetly peeked into it; there was a website with a curious logo of a roaring tiger's head with a hissing venomous jet-black snake snaking its way across the tiger's torso and emerging at its throat. The two animals seemed to be attacking something together, which was absurd. Since when do tigers and snakes hunt the same thing? Ahan entered Pooja's name in the search engine. Around twenty suggestions popped up.

He looked up at Pooja, embarrassed, clearing his throat, "What is your last name?"

"Bahl," Pooja answered.

He researched her name and opened a file. It had all the details about her life—her relatives' names, her friends' names, her vacations—everything was listed in it. On the top was a picture of her, the same picture used in her official documents; it had her name, birthday, and another category named status, which had a big, red stamp that read 'summon'.

"Well, it is pretty clear. The base is expecting you, Bahl."

"Wait, what base? Are you stalking me? How do you have this information? Why do you have this information?"

"To answer your last question, Pooja, it is because you are one of the lucky humans on Earth and have been blessed by the Hindu gods to protect our world from the asuras." He turned away, stuffing the tab into his pack.

"You're joking, right?" Pooja shut her mouth, which had fallen open.

Ahan grinned, "Nope."

MY REAL SPIRIT ANIMAL- I GUESS THE QUIZZES WERE WRONG

"Gods," repeated Pooja for the thirtieth time that day, "Hindu gods?"

"Yes," Ahan sighed.

After revealing the shocking news, Ahan calmly asked Pooja to follow him out of the school and opened the door of his car. It was a blue Kia, ordinary, unlike Pooja's life events. Ahan was driving with Mahi sitting next to him. Pooja made herself as comfortable as she dared in the back seat.

"I don't understand anything," Pooja exhaled.

"Don't you worry, we have a huge PowerPoint presentation waiting for you back at the base."

"Ugh," groaned Pooja, "I cannot focus on PPTs. Can you explain in brief?"

"Right, I'll just excuse you and make an exception."

"Thanks."

"What?" Ahan sighed resignedly. "Well, most of the Hindu gods were mortal once upon a time. Sometimes the BVMs even took up forms as mortals."

"BVMs?"

"Brahma, Vishnu, and Maheshwar. Anyways, obviously, since the devas exist, so do the asuras; it's the universe's way of balancing things. The gods live a life of dharma where they have no direct involvement on Earth, so they pick a few special humans who have roots in India and give them some of their powers; these humans dedicate their lives to fight the asuras." He glanced at his wife before continuing, "Some don't do what they are meant to, like Prajwal. You will learn about him later. The humans blessed by the respective gods will get some of their power. For instance, Mahi was blessed by Lord Yama, so she has some control over the dead. She can summon ghosts and communicate with them, which is beyond cool and helpful. The gods are also in continuous war with the asuras. We are their army on Earth. When the time is right, we get summoned to the base, and we spend the rest of our lives training for the Final War; if it happens in your lifetime."

"What will the war do?"

"The war will end Kaliyuga and begin Satya-yuga."

"Oh. What exactly do you mean by training for the war? Are there, like, specific roles each of us get when we graduate from our training or something?"

"Oh, yeah. We train for battle while learning skills like decoding codes, human resource management, math, chemical reactions, and so on. You can either pick to teach new kids in the base, do fieldwork, be in the main army, work in the court, or be a recruiter. The teachers live in the base with full protection, teaching the newcomers based on the skills they excel at. Like, Mahi would be teaching History in the base school, where you will learn about the gods instead of the French Revolution and all that. Fieldwork consists of undercover missions, like James Bond, but magical."

"Percy Jackson?"

"Yeah, kind of. People working in the main army are classified into generals, cavalry, archers, spearmen, etc. They are for protection in case of an emergency and, of course, are our main hope in the Final War. When the War comes, everybody has to fight, but the main army will be the first ones to charge and the rest will be backup. There is a democratic court that manages the smooth flow of everything. In this court, you can work as the minister, the secretary, and so on. If you work as a recruiter, like Mahi and I, you will have regular jobs and live in the regular world. We will notice people that we think are blessed by gods; they will have an aura that we recruiters are trained to sense. When identified, we protect them and take them to the base. Mahi was about to take you this weekend, actually, but the plan got ruined." He sucked in his breath and shrugged, like 'What are we going to do about it?'

"You're a recruiter?"

"Yeah."

"But Mahi ma'am told me that you were an HR at a company."

"Well, sometimes people's auras are so weak, they are not prominent until adulthood. We call them the Next Generation, basically the descendants of the kids of the Blessed and normal humans. Most of the time, Blesseds live at the Base with their Blessed kids who can have the powers of their parents combined. You will meet a lot of them."

"I'm a Blessed, right?"

"Yeah."

"What kind am I?"

"The Blessed kids' kind, I guess. We call them the Mixes if the parents are Blessed by two different gods. It's advised to marry people of the same power because the kids' power would be stronger. They are also known as the Blessed."

"Is it so for me?"

"Honestly, most of your information has been hidden. You're definitely important."

"Have you recruited before?"

"Yeah."

"Um, did something like Thalia happen?"

"Sometimes, yeah."

"Are you always so blunt when you reveal that we are God's chosen or whatever?"

"Yeah, I mean, a guy's gotta have some fun, no?" Ahan winked. Mahi lightly slapped his hand, laughing.

Ahan stopped the car suddenly. Pooja looked around, there was nothing special about the place, just a normal road in Hyderabad. She noticed Ahan and Mahi getting out and scrambled out herself. As soon as she stepped out of the car, she inhaled sharply in wonder.

"A forest in Hyderabad?" Pooja breathed in awe.

The entrance to what could only be a massive forest was absolutely enchanting. The lush green leaves and colorful flowers intertwined to form a gate–like structure, welcoming the party of three with soft green grass spread like a carpet on the forest floor.

"You can only see this if you have the gods' blessing," Ahan said, breaking the comfortable silence.

"Of course," muttered Pooja, she noticed that Ahan was holding three backpacks in his hands.

Ahan noticed her looking at them and informed, "These are all the essential items we need to reach the base."

"Do you always have so many on hand?" Pooja wondered, looking into the trunk of the car filled with the same pale blue backpacks Ahan was holding.

"Yes," Ahan simply stated before handing Pooja and Mahi their bags.

They set course and entered the forest, which became even more breathtaking as they went deeper. There were enough trees in the first ten meters alone that could make Hyderabad greener than the Amazon rainforest, and Pooja absolutely loved it. After the day's traumatic events, this forest calmed her and proved to be a fantastic distraction. She felt safe in nature this was the time she could use some comfort and safety. Pooja couldn't help but notice the absence of other forms of life. A lush forest like this would usually be filled with fauna, except this, she guessed.

After walking for a while, the sun slowly began to sink lower. Ahan suggested they should make camp and settle in for the night.

"Wait, for the night? How long will it take for us to reach the base?" Pooja asked.

"Well, if we go by this route, two weeks tops," Ahan answered.

"There is another route? How long will that take?"

"We will reach by tomorrow evening."

"Why can't we take that route?"

"We are not allowed there, Pooja. It is not safe. It's better to stay on this path," Mahi warned, plopping herself down on a log and arranging her backpack near her feet. "All animals stay there, prey and predator."

"Don't be so serious," Ahan smiled softly, sitting next to his wife and draping his arm around her. She rested her face on his chest and closed her eyes; all her worry seemed to have been sucked out. Pooja felt extremely uncomfortable, not wanting to intrude on their private moment. She quickly left to find some dry leaves and wood to start a campfire. She felt a hot rush of anger at how content Mahi was after losing someone she apparently loved to talk to – Thalia – although she probably only tolerated her friends to get closer to Pooja to take her to the base. That's all she was to her, just a job, a mission. If they made it back to the base, she would just be a job well done; maybe she'd get promoted. Great.

After assuring Ahan and Mahi that she wouldn't venture far, she roamed around, trying to get Thalia's face out of her head. When she ventured into a clearing, her skin prickled; she felt a predator's gaze on her. She cursed softly; the bag had a knife, and she had left it. She froze, legs and hands apart, ready to fight back or run for her life. Slowly, she turned, looking for a sign to spot the hiding place of the predator. She heard bushes softly rustling to her left; she whipped her head and found herself face to face with a tiger. This tiger was at least thrice the size of Pooja, with biceps bigger than Pooja's body. Its teeth were sharp blades with drool dripping from them, its nose sniffing the air around Pooja. Its eyes were sharp and calculating, but not evil. Its dark orbs took in Pooja and slowly began to approach her. Pooja did not feel scared anymore; she felt safer than she had. Out of instinct, she reached out and placed her hand between the tiger's eyes. Do not try this at home.

"Simba," the name came to her as if it were always there, on the tip of her tongue.

'Pooja,' the tiger's royal voice whispered in her head, 'I missed you.'

"You can talk?" Pooja asked, bewildered, but her voice came out louder than she meant it to. She heard crashing from the path she took, and a few seconds later, Ahan and Mahi appeared, weapons drawn.

"Are you okay?" Ahan asked, uncertain, looking at Pooja petting the tiger.

"Yes," Pooja confirmed, "This is my tiger, Simba."

"Oh, I see." Ahan did not seem surprised; he flicked his sword, turning it back into a ring. Sword rings seemed to be in fashion. "You met your guide."

"Guide?"

"Yeah, every single blessed one has an animal companion that will come to you and stay with you, physically and mentally, until you die. Once you die, it dies too, and you both are burned together. The animal you are given matches your soul; Mahi's is a wolf, like Lord Yama's pets."

"Yes, it matches the soul," Mahi chuckled, "That's why yours is a monkey."

"It is?" Pooja giggled.

"Yep."

"Of course not, mine's a tiger. Bhudevi did give birth to Lord Narasimha, and I got the lion," Ahan informed, pouting.

Mahi laughed, ruffling his hair and kissing him lightly on the nose. Pooja turned her attention back to the tiger.

"You are magnificent," she whispered.

'I am blushing,' the tiger said, face serious. It stretched itself and began to speak, out loud this time, "Ahan Singh, I will help you reach the base faster. My pride will stay with you guys to keep you safe from…others."

"The guide path?" Mahi gasped in disbelief. "I thought you could not enter there."

"Wait, the guide path? Was it this path you warned me about?" Pooja asked.

Everybody ignored her.

"Not on your own, but with another guide, for sure."

From the same bushes Simba had emerged, an ambush of twenty tigers followed, some holding wood in their mouths, while some deer.

"Thought you could use some help," Simba shrugged, leading the ambush back to their camp.

Within half an hour, there was a blazing fire on which Mahi was roasting the deer. Pooja and Simba were snuggled together, Pooja pestering him with questions as he ignored her, grooming himself while Ahan was preparing the tents.

Simba's pride disappeared into the woods, but Pooja could still feel their presence.

"Dinner is ready," Mahi announced, serving the food onto three plates.

Ahan and Pooja approached her and took their share. Pooja poked the food uncertainly with her finger.

"It's delicious, don't worry," Ahan chuckled at the grossed-out look on her face.

"You're only saying that because your wife cooked this," Pooja countered.

"I can and am taking offense," Mahi scoffed in mock annoyance.

Pooja took a tentative bite and saw that Ahan was right. Her taste buds more or less exploded in joy. Pooja did not realize how hungry she was. She devoured her food and licked her hand clean. She looked up to see Mahi giving her a told-you-so look. Pooja smiled and excused herself to go to her tent. It was dark as the night for camouflage, small, with an inflatable mattress, sheets, and a pillow. This setup reminded Pooja of the simpler times when she went camping with her family. As she lay on the mattress, her thoughts drifted to her parents.

Pooja wondered if her parents knew where she was, and then she wondered if they even noticed she wasn't home. Pooja liked to disappear for hours because her home was her personal hell. She tried not to feel guilty about her feelings of extreme relief of leaving her house for good. When Ahan had told her that she would have to spend the rest of her life at the base, she felt extremely happy, even though it was basically a military camp. She just hoped her parents couldn't visit her as she was apparently "important."

She was elated that she did not have to go back to her life where her father came home drunk every night and beat her mercilessly and tried to make up to her by taking her out every weekend. She did not want to go back to her mother who justified her father's cruel behavior since Pooja was a child, convincing her that fathers did worse to their children and she was lucky to have such a good one. She did not even realize the abuse she was going through until she went to Thalia's house for a sleepover, where her family was actually happy, not pretending for the guests. Pooja closed her eyes tightly, not letting the tears rapidly filling them fall.

Soon, Pooja drifted off into an uneasy sleep, her dreams playing Thalia's death on repeat. She felt trapped in her dreams like she did in real life, unable to do anything as the arrow pierced her friend's gut. She could only imagine Thalia's reaction as her brain realized what had happened. 'Because you weren't there for her final moments,' a nasty voice said in her head, 'Even though she was always there for you.'

Pooja was woken up at the crack of dawn by Simba, who licked her face clean. Pooja took out the toiletries packed in her bag and got ready. Mahi and Ahan greeted her sleepily, dark circles under their eyes proving they didn't get enough sleep. They quickly ate the last night's cold leftovers, which tasted horrible, and set out again to the base.

As they entered the guide path, Pooja felt the mood shift. While the path they had been taking before was welcoming and beautiful, this one seemed dangerous. The air was thick with danger, and Pooja's senses were on high alert. They walked one path and moved at a steady speed. Pooja had a feeling that they were not being ambushed only because of Simba's presence and his ambush.

"I have to ask," Pooja began. "You said that the guides would be there until the person dies, right? But don't animals hunt each other, and hence kill each other as well?"

"Very few animals are guides," Ahan informed. "This forest connects all the forests of the world, the mortal one included. This is how we can travel from one place to another so quick. This also helps the predators hunt the normal animals for nourishment. Food webs and all."

"So, there are Blessed animals?" Pooja let out an incredulous laugh.

"Pretty much, it's a great honor," Ahan frowned at her.

By the time they had reached the base, it was almost midnight. The first thing they saw was the gate. It was at least twenty feet high, armed with multiple defensive mechanisms. A group of wild animals like lions, tigers, wolves, and cheetahs stood guard. Among the animals were two heavily armed and muscular guards in black combat gear.

"Stop right there," a guard commanded, "and state your purpose."

"I am Ahan Javed Singh. I am here with Mahi Singh; we are part of the recruitment team. We have Pooja Bahl with us," Ahan held up his hands.

"Let them in with full honors," a voice rang. Pooja's eyes flicked to the man approaching the gate from inside.

He had a confident smile, warm brown eyes that looked stern and soft at the same time, a chiseled jaw, and military-style cropped dark hair. He stood tall and bold, dressed in sweeping black and silver clothes with the same logo on the tablet printed on the breast of his robe.

"Come on in, then. We have a lot to talk about."

Pooja fell in step with Ahan as they walked toward the castle. It was a five-hundred-meter walk to the main palace; many beautiful trees and fountains decorated the path. If they had arrived in the morning, they would have heard sounds of combat nearby and noticed a combat area where people learn sword fighting. Next to them was the archery range, the mace training compartment, and many more physical activities. To the right was a sandy beach with a lighthouse on the right. There was a huge wall separating the main castle walls from the beach. The whole place made her dizzy with déjà vu. She knew for sure that she had visited this place before, but it felt like the memory was physically removed from her head.

The castle itself was beautifully built. It radiated power and elegance like the man they were following. It was huge, the end disappearing into the sky with four sub-compartments. They walked to the main castle and spilled into a beautiful hall. It was decorated with chandeliers and torch brackets, casting a warm, golden light around the room. It looked like a palace fit for the Pandavas to reside in, with a touch of modern technology and the scent of magic in the air. There were extremely comfortable sofas on which many people were sitting. As soon as the party entered, the chatter stopped, and everyone stood up in respect. They turned left, ignoring the main desk where a couple of people were lined up, and into a corridor.

They climbed into the most luxurious lift ever. It had red velvet carpets on the ground and was made out of pure gold with extremely complex mechanisms for defense and escape. The base reminded Pooja of a safe house in the middle of a war, except it was a huge castle, obviously developed over many centuries.

Faster than Pooja expected, they reached the chamber of the king. Pooja knew because it said 'Chamber of the King' on the door. It flung open as soon as the man they were following touched it, who could only be the king. They walked into a room that was in shades of purple. Velvety purple carpets, royal purple and golden chairs, light violet walls with paintings of the Pandavas, Krishna, the King, and others who were obviously ancestors. Even in the paintings, they had the same dark hair and authoritative aura around them.

There was a black desk behind which the king sat.

"I am the acting king of the world, Indra. I am not the God, Devendra, ruler of the gods, but a normal man," he winked. "I normally don't welcome people personally, but this time it is an exception as..."

"You know me," Pooja interrupted. It was probably rude to interrupt, but after all the traumatic events she went through, her respecting skills were rusty. Not too rusty, though, she quickly added, "I am sorry to interrupt, Mr Indra, but I really am sick and tired of this. I am sure I have interacted with you and your world thanks to this ring, my talking tiger, and Prajwal's statements. I could really use a proper explanation right now."

"Of course. I will explain everything in detail."

He then sent them to the guest rooms in the palace to freshen up followed by dinner because 'news is well digested after a stomach full of food.'

Pooja was more than happy to oblige even though she still wanted the promised answers. She filled a tub with hot water and stepped into it, washing off all the mud, dirt, and blood from her body. She felt extremely relaxed, and thoughts of Thalia entered her head. She opened her eyes and quickly put remorse aside; she needed answers first; she could grieve later.

She finished bathing and stepped out, feeling fresh and clean again. She dressed in the clothes that were laid out for her on her bed and went down to the dining room with lots of assistance from the staff, getting lost thrice. She sat next to Mahi who was waiting for the royal family to arrive. Ahan gave her a nod, acknowledging her presence, and she nodded back; this place felt like an official meeting rather than a dinner.

At last, the royal family arrived, fashionably late, of course. These people were very humble. A beautiful woman was holding the hand of the acting king; she had glossy black hair that tumbled down to her waist, and she wore minimal makeup and jewelry, but she had the eyes of all the men in the room, except for Ahan, who was pointedly looking away. Her royal violet gown swept the floor, and she gracefully made her way to the table. She was probably in her forties but did not look a day older than twenty-three; she looked at Pooja and gave her a dazzling smile that made a lot of servants tumble and fall.

Pooja clamped her mouth shut to avoid laughing out loud.

Behind the couple were two boys who could only be twins. They both had the same smile, face shape, and walking style. They were both wearing navy blue suits with a cream shirt and no tie. The one to the left had wavy hair and electric blue eyes, while the other had ruler-straight hair with brown eyes.

"Hello, Pooja. Long time no see," the queen smiled, her sweet voice making the other servants drool, and Pooja's attention snapped to her. "You might not remember me, but I am Ayesha."

"Hello," she said.

"Kamadev blessed the queen," Mahi whispered to her.

It made sense, Kamadev was the god of love in Hindu mythology. His job was to make two people fall in love, like Cupid. He was extremely attractive, making him the centre of attention in every room. Clearly that was passed down to Ayesha.

The family seated themselves near the head of the table. The king sat at the head, the queen to his left next to Pooja, and the princes opposite her. The blue-eyed one, who was sitting opposite her, leaned forward, "Hello, I am Arjun Thakur and this is my brother, Avi. It is nice to finally meet you."

"*Finally* meet me?"

"Yeah. Dad has been talking about you since you arrived. He was not exaggerating anything," his eyes roamed around her face.

"I see," Pooja got distracted as the waiters began to serve steaming biryani onto her plate. She began to stuff her face. The first bite of the food brought tears to her eyes; it was amazing. She could tell the chef cooked it with love and passion.

"So, you like the food I made, I take it," Arjun chuckled politely.

Pooja looked at him, wide-eyed, "You made this?"

"Yeah, I did. Dad was talking about making you feel comfortable here and I guess I thought food would bring you comfort. I heard about your friend. I am sorry."

"How did you hear about my friend? Also, will you cook for me every day?"

"My dad had a chat with Ahan after you left to freshen up. Obviously, I won't cook for you every day?" Arjun laughed.

"What if I married you?" Pooja blurted out and then cringed internally. She wished she would stop saying stupid things like that sometimes.

"Then, I will. I will cook, clean, and look pretty for you when you get back from work."

"What?" Pooja asked, a spoonful of biryani hovering near her mouth.

Arjun and Avi laughed at her bemused expression; Pooja joined in. Soon, the three of them were hysterically laughing as the adults looked at them.

"These are the kids we raised," Ayesha sighed dramatically.

They finished eating, and Indra took the kids and Ayesha up to his chamber after telling Ahan and Mahi to rest. They left as though glad to be gone, leaving Pooja to trail behind the stranger, his wife, and kids, telling herself that she was fine.

After they made themselves comfortable, Indra cleared his throat and began, "Well, here is everything you need to know."

DIVING INTO THE PAST AND HITTING THE BOTTOM – HARD

Long ago, in Dwapar Yuga, after the Mahabharat war was over and everything began to calm down, Shri Krishna went to visit his dear friend Sudhama. Sudhama was incredibly sick and was in his last days; his old, wrinkly body lay on a plush cot, pillows supporting him. Krishna arrived and sat with Sudhama; it was just like old times, but not quite. Krishna still looked young, his rich, dark skin accentuating his beauty. His eyes were deep and filled with concern as he gazed at his childhood friend, feeling his life force slowly slip away.

Sudhama noticed this and asked, "Why are you worried, Krishna?"

"Oh, Sudhama," Krishna replied, "I see your life is ending. I regret not spending enough time with you."

At that, Sudhama laughed, "Krishna, you are the Paramatma. You are ubiquitous. You exist in every living and non-living thing in this whole world. You are within me, my wife, my children, even the clothes I wear. But that is not your primary concern, what is it?"

Krishna sighed, "Sudhama, they destroyed the world as it is."

"Why must this concern you, Krishna?"

"The world as we know it will not exist anymore. The yuga will end, and there will be no proper ruler in Kaliyuga," Krishna admitted sadly.

"Krishna, your descendants would make great rulers of the world," Sudhama replied with a soft, bemused smile.

"My descendants will not exist, Sudhama," Krishna's eyes filled with pain as he gave his friend a sad smile.

"What are you saying?" Sudhama gasped in horror.

"Yes, all of my children will die."

In utter disbelief, Sudhama asked, " What will you do about this?"

Krishna pursed his lips, "Kaliyuga is not fair. It is treacherous and most difficult. It will judge the gods, and it can make them fall. In these times, there will be an increased need for a proper ruler for the world. There will be monsters eager to end Kaliyuga in hopes that they can rule the world instead of letting the cycle of the yugas continue. The scary thing is that it could happen; they could succeed. For this scenario, the world needs a leader capable of letting the universe run on its own rules. I have thought about it for a long time and have come to a decision. Sudhama, my friend, I trust you completely and have decided that one of your descendants will be the one to restore order in our world. There will be a time in Kaliyuga when a boy and a girl from your family will be born in the same year. These kids will be born with special powers as my blessings, and they will slowly unravel these in their journey."

"I am honored, but what about the Pandavas?"

Krishna smiled his mischievous smile, "You would be proud to know that your great-granddaughter had just the charm to get the attention of a certain Pandav prince's descendant."

"The Pandav prince is Arjun?" asked Sudhama, smiling a weak but happy smile.

"Arjun," Krishna confirmed, slipping a bracelet off his hand, "Pass this down to your descendants. When the time comes for the rulers to be born, this will glow."

That night, Sudhama's soul left his body happily.

....

"Any questions?" asked Indra.

Pooja, Avi, and Arjun were staring at him, mouths open. They closed them quickly.

"I am Sudhama's descendant?" Pooja asked.

"Yes, but not directly. Your family tree is long and complicated."

"So, I have to get married to Pooja?" Arjun asked, slowly.

"Or I do," Avi said, quickly flashing a smile at Pooja that made her blush and then scowl.

"That was the theory, but as you have heard, the word 'marriage' does not appear in Lord Krishna's blessing to Sudhama."

"That is good because this means Arjun, Avi, and I are cousins," Pooja grimaced.

Indra threw his head back, laughing. "Pooja, this happened hundreds of years ago. Your blood relation is very thin. If you look at it that way, you are cousins of everyone in this world."

"Who exactly should rule, Father? Me or Avi?" Arjun asked.

"That is a good question, Arjun. We don't know."

"Well, this could also mean that the time did not come for the Prince and Princess, right?" Pooja suggested.

"No, no, it is definitely the time. Let me tell you the story of when the bracelet finally glowed.

"Since the demise of Sudhama, his descendants have made it a point to stay in contact with each other. These Brahmans were admitted into the court of Indraprastha with Krishna's recommendation. Sure enough, the families never had a male and female child in the same year. Like Lord Krishna said, Sudhama's great-granddaughter married Janamejaya.

"Just as things were looking up, there were a lot of rebellions throughout the kingdom, blaming King Yudhishtir for his lack of mindset and ability to be a rightful king. Enraged at the preposterous claims, Janamejaya's descendants began fighting wars against them. Alas, a lot of the army agreed with the rebels and joined them, so they were slaughtered."

"What? Why would they agree that Yudhishtir was anything but a right, just king?" Arjun asked sceptically.

"Probably because he gambled his wife away," Pooja snapped, shrugging. "Just saying."

"That's a deep discussion. Many layers led to him making that choice," Ayesha replied.

"The only layer I see is a king who made millions of people miserable because he misinterpreted dharma," Pooja retorted.

"Actually," Arjun began, facing her with a frown on his beautiful face, his forehead scrunching with the action.

"Oh, stop it," Avi interjected. "Knowing my brother, you two will be arguing about this 'til the end of time!"

Arjun glared at his brother, who glared right back before turning to their father. "So, how are we still alive then?"

"Well, a few remaining men, Harsheya and Drashadev, escaped the wrath of the rebels. Harsheya and Drashadev were the descendants of Janamjeya with Sudhama's daughter. They were the two princes who set up this secret facility. This facility was meant to work in the background and keep the world balanced while ensuring all the descendants of Sudhama were there within the facility," Indra answered.

"It's a truly beautiful concept," Pooja agreed. "But then there was the matter of the Delhi Sultanate that took over our country. How did this facility thrive?"

"That's a good question, Pooja. During those times, the facility *did* threaten to collapse, but our ancestors kept it together." He gestured to a painting of a man to his left - a king with green eyes as striking as her father's and a beard to rival Aquaman. "We became stronger after that?" Pooja enquired.

"Of course we did, we are blessed by *gods*. The Delhi Sultanate or the Mughals couldn't touch us. We learnt about this in our History class a couple of years ago," Arjun replied.

"So how come you didn't help when the Britishers invaded our lands?" Pooja scoffed.

"Well," Arjun spluttered. "Mortals make their own mistakes. We don't interfere in their little matters."

"*Little* matters? The Bengal Famine, caused by the British, killed *millions* of people. I learnt about that *this* year. What is the point of such powerful beings if you don't defend the defenceless? How are you helping society?" Pooja raged.

"We will help society when it matters the most," Ayesha interjected. "Defeating the asuras and ensuring that the Wheel of Time, or the Kalachakra, goes as planned. We must conserve our strength and gifts from the gods to fulfill our life's mission. This will save billions."

"Kalachakra? Like the four yugas?" Pooja asked.

"Yes, Satya, Treta, Dwapara, and Kali yugas," Indra guided the conversation back to him.

"I think we're straying from the 'glowing bracelet' thing," Avi said. "We should probably get back to that."

"Absolutely. The 'secret facility' was renamed as the 'Base' and has been developing since. Harsheya and Drashdev created a tradition where their kids would all compete when they came of age to decide who would rule. Of course, until the whole 'glowing bracelet' phenomenon. Many centuries later, I was born as Harsheya's descendant. Pooja's father, Jayanth, as Drashdev's. We were the best of friends and trained hard, each receiving the same education.

When we turned eighteen, we were both were put through a series of challenges to determine who the acting king would be, which was our tradition. As you can tell, I passed the test and continued my studies as the acting king and Jayanth as the trusted adviser, my right-hand man."

"Hold on, you knew my dad?" Pooja asked. "How come he's never mentioned you?"

Indra's eyes turned sad. "Your father was one of the best men I've known in my life. However, the world is not perfect. Things changed between us—a lot. Jayanth's father, Ram, wanted his son to rule and was extremely disappointed in him. This ruined your father, who strived to prove himself to your grandfather. He became ruthless and harsh, eventually causing an irreparable gap in our friendship."

"He was the best man you knew? What kind of people did you grow up with?" Pooja laughed.

Ayesha looked at her with pity, "The man you know is not the same man that my husband loved like a brother."

"Good to know," Pooja frowned, reaching to pet Simba, curled at her feet. "Let's talk about when we were born?"

"Time skip to 2005," Indra continued, "When both of us got married to the women who literally took our breath away - Jaya and Ayesha. Ayesha was eye-catching, Blessed by Kamadev. She had every man begging to be hers but she chose me. I couldn't be more grateful or happier. Jaya was the light in Jayanth's dark world. She lit up his face with a joy I hadn't seen since before I became king. We were truly happy with whom we married, and I saw hope that we could repair our ruined relationships," he paused, drinking deeply from a glass of water to hide the tears forming in his eyes."Let me take it from here," Ayesha interjected to save her husband. "Two years later, both Jaya and I were expecting. We visited the bracelet in our sacred temple, which was shining with divine light as we entered. We couldn't have been happier. Unfortunately, in the second month of Jaya's pregnancy, she lost the baby, crushing the hopes of us and our citizens. Jayanth's father was livid and blamed Jaya for being careless with the baby and destroying hope for our lands. He influenced Jayanth to believe the same and hate the person whom he loved with a burning passion. I, on the other hand, delivered a healthy baby girl, Aadhya, a couple of months later. This made the scenario worse for my friend."

"Yeah, let's not go into details," Pooja muttered, attempting to pull her sleeves in to hide the scars decorating her wrists and snaking up to her arms—the souvenirs from her childhood.

"Then, in 2009, we were both expecting at the same time, again," Ayesha hurriedly continued. "This filled our hearts with hope and joy. It made Jayanth a better man once again. I gave birth to two beautiful baby boys. We named one Arjun and the other Avi. Two male guide snakes hatched on the same day, at the same time, and were delivered to my babies.

"We realised that the male ruler was never meant to be the oldest child. Lord Krishna never said he had to be, so we were still hopeful. In around four months, Jaya gave birth to Pooja. A guide tiger dropped off its cub in her crib. We were convinced that these were the three who made the world a better place to live in. Everything looked fine again; everyone was fine again. Unfortunately, we did not know who the Prince was here, but we weren't too worried."

"So, we grew up together?" Avi asked.

"For a while," Ayesha chuckled, recalling their early childhood. "You three were close as anything when you were babies, though you were complete opposites. Pooja was a violent child who could, even as a baby, cause some *serious* injuries."

Pooja flashed her teeth at the boys who just stared at her with a mixture of amusement and fear.

Ayesha gave her the stink eye. "Arjun was the silent one, the most disciplined. Avi used to hang around, cutely biting people's hands for fun. You three made a dangerous trio, getting anything you wanted from anyone.

"We have a campus attached to this castle where you three used to roam around whenever you wanted. We had no problem with this. Arjun and Avi were cautious kids who never used to go anywhere, but Pooja was an adventurous one. That was why one day, Pooja randomly crawled into a history class as if she owned the place. She crawled to the teacher's dais, curled up, and slept with her tiger next to her. The tiger would growl at her whenever the teacher tried to pick her up. Since animals were sacred to us, she did not dare to hurt him."

"Sounds like me," Pooja admitted. "We had a lot of fun, didn't we? Me and Simbha?"

"Oh yeah, the amount of chaos you two created," Indra shook his head with a smile. "The whole Base was your playground, and us your playthings."

"You did calm down, though," Ayesha told her. "That day itself, a bright, young student, Mahi, walked up to the dais and approached the tiger. It sniffed Mahi and concluded she wasn't a threat to the sleeping Pooja. The tiger did not react as she gently pulled the baby into her arms. Pooja woke up and cuddled closer to her. Ahan, one of Mahi's closest friends, walked up to her, snatched the baby from her hands, and spun her around. Pooja, jerking awake, screamed in delight, babbling, then resting her head on his chest. Prajwal, Mahi's boyfriend, walked toward the front and chided them both for messing with the baby. He picked Pooja up and had her safely get back to her nursery."

"Prajwal?" Pooja exclaimed. "You mean ugly, receding hairline Prajwal? The one who tried to kill me?"

"Yeah, that's the one," Indra confirmed.

"Ew, I was close with that vermin?" Pooja gagged.

"Real close with the whole lot of them," Indra smiled at his wife.

"The three students would not leave Pooja and her tiger alone. They loved caring for and entertaining her. The bond the four of them had was strong and unbreakable. Both Mahi and Prajwal were brilliant students, so we were considering making them part of Pooja's official bodyguards. At that time, they did not even know she was the Princess, destined to save them. We were incredibly delighted, believing the universe was setting the path for its saviors."

"So, when did you guys realize that Prajwal wasn't a good guy?" Avi asked.

"One day, Mahi was taking care of Pooja, casually playing with her, when she heard it. Alarms were blaring, calling for an emergency meeting. There was a security breach, which meant it was protocol for everyone to drop everything they were doing and gather, disciplined at the Assembly Point," Ayesha began.

"Like a fire drill?" Pooja asked.

"Yeah, except more intense, us being Blessed and all," Ayesha winked.

"Right, sorry," Pooja gestured to Ayesha to continue.

"Let me, since I was there," Indra placed a hand on his wife's. "I climbed onto the stage and projected the CCTV footage on the screen. CCTVs were a thing here; we are always ahead of human technology due to our magic. Prajwal Borkar hacked into the security system; he tried to make an invasion of Asuras happen. Unfortunately for him, he underestimated our defensive strategies. The moment he hacked into the system, it relocked itself, giving only Prajwal time to get out, ruining his plan. I told this to everyone and called his friends to my office."

"So, they *were* conspiring with him?" Avi asked, shocked.

"Obviously not, you idiot," Arjun slapped his forehead.

"Language," Indra said tightly. "But Arjun's right, a mind reader confirmed the same as Ahan was trying to prove his innocence."

"You were interrogating them, then? So, you just let me be with them without knowing their pasts?" Pooja scoffed.

"Of course not, Ahan and Mahi come from well respected families in our Base. Prajwal, however, was a direct descendant of a soldier who tried to save our ancestor's life. He is known as the Last Hope. He and the other descendants of Sudhama found themselves in a sticky situation with the Mughals. The other descendant died from blood loss, and it seemed like the other would as well. Prajwal Borkar the First tried to save his life and was nearly successful. The world thought the two descendants died without heirs, but it was proved wrong. Prajwal had the gift of seeing the future, so he married the other descendant and sired an heir with her against her parents' will. He also wrote down the exact location he hid his and the Last Hope's child and left it in his coat pocket for us to find. He saved our whole generation."

"That's why everyone trusted the ugly Prajwal. That made it easy for him to betray us all," Avi fumed.

"But why the hell would he do that?" Pooja wondered.

"Language," Indra chided, before replying, "That's the greatest mystery of all."

"So, what happened with Ahan and Mahi the day Prajwal betrayed us?" Arjun asked.

"Well, we told them that Pooja was the Princess and we had to erase their memories because they would be a liability when it comes to protecting her."

"Why?" Pooja rolled her eyes. "Wouldn't it be *better* if Prajwal's friends protected me? It would be harder for him to kill them."

"True, but your parents were too spooked that you were so close to a traitor. They believed it would be better if you lived in the human world," Ayesha answered.

"That's stupid!" Pooja exclaimed. "They just wanted to abandon the world?"

"They cared for you," Ayesha reasoned.

"Cared?" Pooja was yelling now. "You let them take me away from a place I was completely safe and comfortable. You *let* him hurt us for *years*."

"We didn't know," Indra began.

"Oh, stop it!" she growled, jumping up to her feet, Simba right behind her. "You have all the resources in the world. You knew I was coming here. You knew *everything*."

"Your father forced us to take an oath not to interfere," Ayesha raised her palms toward Pooja.

Pooja felt the rage and hatred in the pit of her stomach, and her eyes burnt as she forced all the emotion out, showing them exactly what she thought of their pathetic excuses.

"Calm down," Indra's firm voice grounded her. The energy that was rapidly building up behind her eyes slowed to a stop, leaving behind a faint headache between her eyes.

She sat down, hiding her face in her hands, taking a few breaths to calm herself. "Did you do it?"

"What?" Indra frowned slightly.

"Erase their memories?" she asked, looking up.

"Yes. If it means anything, they put up a huge fight. They didn't want to let you go at all. They loved you dearly," Indra smiled softly.

'Her father took that love away from her' was what she wanted to say, but Pooja just nodded.

"We purged your memories too, and locked your magic so you could live a normal life," Indra continued.

"How did you do it? My whole family has been living here. How can they live outside the Base?" Another thought struck her, quick and sharp as lightning. "Why do you even need recruiters when everyone lives here?"

"I'll answer all your questions," Indra confirmed. "Your father always had a steady flow of money to keep you all comfortable. The Base uses the mortal world to gather information about the asuras. He pretended to run a business that we own."

"As for the recruiters," Ayesha chewed her lip, "Some Blessed left the Base when the magic wore thin in their blood. Some just weren't lucky enough to be Blessed. However, their children inherit powers through genetics, and we take them in. We emphasized recruiting for these few years so that we could find you one day."

"So, you wanted me here to save the world?" Pooja said slowly.

"We do," Indra nodded. "But the choice is yours. You have the power here, kid. You can choose to return to the mortal world or live here, learn our ways, and fulfill your destiny. You coming here is a great blessing, the sign of change and better times for our citizens. The Princess' return is something to be celebrated, a sign of strength, which is desperately required in these dire circumstances. My intel tells me that Prajwal is mobilizing an army, maybe helping, or leading the asuras. Prajwal could've been trying to recruit Pooja today, which is terrifying. The prospect of having the Prince and Princess against each other is going to send the world into utter chaos. Our situation was bad, so bad we were planning for a scenario where we would lose the war. We need our leaders, and it can't be a coincidence you arrived today when I had lost all hope, and was planning to warn and educate our citizens about the possibility of death."

Pooja contemplated the choice in front of her. She felt as if the gods themselves were holding their breaths, awaiting her decision that would change the course of the world. She didn't even have a place to go back to. Her entire world had collapsed because of Prajwal, and gods be damned if she didn't take the revenge her friend deserved.

"I'll stay here. I want my memories back. I want to stay and help you guys," Pooja decided.

"That's not up to you to decide." That voice. The voice that haunted her dreams, the voice that hurt Pooja, cut deep into her in ways she couldn't imagine. The voice belonged to a man who, as the universe cruelly decided, had the same face as her. She was the mirror image of her nightmare. Every time she looked in the mirror, she saw *him*. Her father. As it always did, it cut her act of bravado into tiny pieces, had her throat close up in fear, and her body tremble against her will.

She scuttled backward, as slowly as possible, praying to all the gods he didn't notice. She scooted toward the shadows, begging them to engulf her and shield her against the first true monster in her life.

His eyes were wild with drunken rage. "Come here, we're going home."

Pooja's body begged her to obey, not wanting to suffer the dire consequences of resisting his commands. She made to approach him, an involuntary reaction.

"No," Indra sternly denied.

"What 'no'? We had an agreement," Jayanth turned on the king, leaving Pooja to scuttle back into the corner and make herself as small as possible.

"Our agreement was that if Pooja is really the princess, fate will bring her back to this castle. Look where we are now. I did not influence anything; I told her the story of Krishna and of Prajwal. She is still in her right mind, well-fed and rested. She is making this decision consciously and you can no longer stop this."

"It is not safe for her," Jayanth, her father's voice rising higher.

"As though it is safe for her out there," Indra's voice met her father's, "Prajwal could have killed her today, or recruited her. Do you know how unsafe that is? Think, Jay, think. Pooja was always meant to be here. Let her embrace her powers and learn to control them. You heard what she did, did you not? She killed twelve extremely trained men, who were more experienced than her, just because her friend was injured! That is something most of my students can only dream of doing. She fits in here; this is her place.”

Killed? Pooja assumed she had knocked them out, not *killed* them. She waited for the dread and the sadness to come. She knew she had to be upset, becoming a murderer at the mere age of thirteen, destroying her innocence by violence and battle. She was stunned at the numbness that greeted her instead.

Truth be told, Pooja was no stranger to battle; she was constantly on a battlefield, adapting to survive. Locked in a mental warfare, battling her harmful and destructive thoughts. Violence was an everyday occurrence in her house and was more familiar to her than love ever was. Pooja was used to violence, and now she thrived in it. It gave her no satisfaction, just left a bitter taste in her mouth. She turned her attention back to the conversation, her head throbbing with all the emotions she was trying to unpack.

“No way, I absolutely forbid this,” Jayanth growled, not used to being disobeyed.

“Pooja,” Indra said gently, “Dear, you can leave with your parents right now, and we won’t question it. We will remove your memories and transfer you to a safer place. Or, you can join us and learn to control your powers.”

“I want to join you,” Pooja firmly repeated, hiding her shaking hands behind her back.

“No!” Jayanth strode toward Pooja, who yelped and pressed herself so close to the wall she was almost *inside* it, raising her hands in defense. Simba stepped in between her and her rapidly advancing father and bared all his sharp and pointy teeth at him, unable to rise to his full height in the closed quarters. As Jayanth reached her, he was flung into the air and crashed against the wall with a satisfying *crack*.

Indra stood next to Pooja, her chair flung aside, his right hand outstretched, fury in his eyes. "Pooja is under my protection now. You will not hurt her. Guards!"

Two bulky men, clad in black armor, entered the room and dragged her parents out. Before they were dragged out of view, Pooja noticed her mother. Her face was as tired and weary as ever. Her once-beautiful face was marred with scars – both physical and emotional. Her body was thin, half a kilogram away from being malnourished. She was wasting away, looking worse than when Pooja last saw her, her hair with more strands of gray, more lines on her forehead. Her eyes, which were usually defeated and dull, were shining with tears and pride. Pride in the choice Pooja had made. It sent a tingle of warmth along her spine, allowing her to stand tall and proud and look her father straight in the eye with defiance.

"Thank you," Pooja weakly murmured to Indra.

"Come now, it's time to restore your memories." Indra's calm demeanor was back.

A few minutes later, Indra and she were in a pearly white room where all Pooja's memories were stored. They accessed the room from a trapdoor under Indra's desk, and his wife and kids opted to stay behind and ensure Pooja's parents left the Base. Or so they claimed; she knew it was for giving her privacy. Pooja stood nervously, intimidated, and blinded by the lights and the people around in lab coats. She could not remember a single thing about being here.

She put her hand on Simba's arm for support as they walked. Every ounce of sleep left her body as they reached a small compartment with a sign reading 'Pooja Bahl.'

Indra pulled open the door and stepped to the side, gesturing for Pooja to go in. Taking a deep breath to calm her nerves, she went inside, hearing the door shut behind her. Immediately, she was enveloped in darkness, the only sound being her heart thumping against her chest. She felt dizzy as her eyes adjusted to this contrast. Suddenly, a white wisp of a substance, much like smoke, floated before her eyes. It flew close and settled on her temple.

Pooja was not in the chamber anymore. She was out in the fields, crawling beside two babies - Arjun and Avi. She crawled next to a horse who had just given birth to three foals. A black one immediately slid next to her, fitting perfectly in her arms.

Another memory, this time next to Mahi as she bit her lip, trying to focus on the test she was writing. Pooja intently stared at the pen as it glided on the paper, writing words. It felt weird and different to her.

Another memory with Prajwal, alone, unlike what Ahan claimed. Prajwal stood close to her, younger with freckles on his face. He looked terrified, messing up his full head of brown curls, mumbling incoherently, "I don't know what to do. I feel like it is embracing me forcefully, taking control of my whole being. I don't want to hurt anyone. Maybe I should have never gone through that damned book. I should've just listened. I want Mahi and Ahan to be safe. They were nothing but kind to me." His eyes bore into Pooja's, haunted yet determined.

"Promise me you will protect them no matter what. I know you can." His voice turned into a snarl. "Promise me!"

Pooja gasped and opened her eyes. She was on the floor of the chamber, the white mist suffocating her as it fought to go back into her head. She closed her eyes and tried to focus on a memory, but there were too many. Screaming, fires, and a massive blast that shook the Earth. One thing she could see most clearly was a face, carved in stone. Long curly hair, flowy mustache, with glowing green eyes as light exited a chamber. This was on a circular door, and a laugh – evil and cruel. Prajwal was standing in front of it. "What have I done?" he asked her, eyes haunted. A sweet voice filled her head, giving her a blissful change from the ominous previous memories. "I love you, kiddo. I always will, and I hope we will find each other again someday." It was Mahi's voice that echoed through her head as her senses deserted her, slowly slipping into the blissful, unconscious state.

AWKWARD CONVERSATIONS FT. AHAN

When Pooja opened her eyes again, she was in a place she did not recognize. Her body was sore, and she realized she was too weak to get up. Not giving up, she forced herself onto one hand and got out of bed. She looked around and registered two things: first, she was back in the guest room where she had her bath. Second, Simba was curled up near the door, looking at her intently.

"Simba!" she exclaimed. "What the hell?"

'You are in your room,' he said unhelpfully.

"That's cool," Pooja glanced at her wrist out of habit, expecting her watch, but then remembered she had forgotten it at home the day before and hadn't received it since, not that she was expecting to. "Um, what's the time?"

'I don't know, look at the watch on the wall,' Simba suggested with a hint of humor. A gothic clock hung on the wall, adding to the vintage yet mysterious vibe of the room. After staring at the fancy numbers for a good moment, Pooja realized it was ten-thirty in the morning. Sighing, she rubbed the exhaustion out of her eyes and went down to the dining room, Simba lazily lying on his back, making no attempts to follow.

This time, the guards stopped her near the entrance. "Apologies," one of them said, "But this room is only for dinners. You must go to the breakfast room, ma'am."

"Oh, right, silly me," Pooja turned around and walked as though she had a purpose, although she did not know where she was going. It seemed like her feet had their own brain because, with a sense of extreme déjà vu, she began to navigate the castle toward the breakfast hall. The first thought that struck her was that the memories she got yesterday were in her head somewhere, and the next was that the king had too much money, as he did not need separate rooms for breakfast, lunch, dinner, and the snack counter. She wondered how she knew about the snack counter.

As soon as she entered the room, the smell of food enveloped her, depriving her of any thought. She plopped down beside Arjun and greeted the royal family with a 'good morning.' Unlike her, everyone was dressed up and eating with dignity and grace.

"Good morning, sleepyhead," Indra greeted her with a smile. "We were just talking about you."

"Obviously, I am the most interesting topic here," she took a bite of idli with a dollop of coconut chutney.

"You will be pleased to know that Mahi and Ahan have also regained their memories last night."

"Pleased to know?" Pooja exclaimed incredulously. "I am overjoyed to know that! Can I meet them... please?" she added as an afterthought.

"Sure, but first we have to sort some things out."

"Like?"

"First of all," Avi began, "To learn here, you have to be chosen into a house. This 'house' is a representation of the god or goddess who has blessed you."

"That was so informative, I did not understand anything."

"What Avi is trying to say is that the houses are classified based on what your powers are and the names are those of gods," Arjun said simply.

"You mean, if my specialty is love, I will be put in the Kamdev house like your mother?"

"Yes," Ayesha replied.

"So, in order to be sorted, do I have to take some tests?"

"Yes. When you were a kid, we performed a holy sacrifice to the gods to find out which gods blessed you. As you guys are not normal, we wanted to know if the blessings worked differently. Sure enough, Arjun and Avi were both blessed by Lord Shiva, and you by Parvati. Lord Shiva specializes in destruction, calmness, high strength, almost invincibility, wisdom..."

"I know, I am a big devotee of him, actually," she replied, producing her rudraksh necklace tucked into her shirt. Even though she didn't believe in gods, she believed in Him. Clutching the Rudraksh always calmed her and made the pain go away.

Ignoring her, Indra continued, "As such, each god or goddess has different strengths, which do coincide with those of other minor gods. Arjun and Avi chose the gods based on their strengths to blend in. Similarly, you will have to blend in with the other students like my children over here and rise to greatness, however cliché that sounded. We want people to respect you, keeping in mind that you have no special training. Your identity will be hidden, and you must make multiple friends so they know you are a normal girl who rose to greatness."

"You are asking me to be a social butterfly?"

"Yes."

"I am an unsocial moth! The only friends I had were Thalia and Anaaya. Now they are gone as well!" Saying it made it real. She realized how much grief she had been holding back, took a deep breath, pushing it deep down. She could not break into tears in front of everyone.

Indra ignored her once more.

"Okay, your tests begin tomorrow," Indra declared, returning to his breakfast.

It turned out that Pooja had arrived just in time for the usually scheduled tests. While all the older members had their finals to test what they learnt the previous year, the new joiners attempted their entrance examinations. Unlike most schools, they had tests on IQ, working under pressure, instincts, survival skills, fitness, combat, and history, which was basically revised mythology.

The whole day was a breeze. Arjun, Avi, and Pooja roamed around the castle, getting to know each other and, in Pooja's case, the castle. Well, re-learnt. Pooja learnt that there were three smaller towers behind the castle: one where all the classes were taken, one for the dormitories, and one for the veterans and teachers. Pooja took her leave and entered the teachers' castle to find Mahi and Ahan.

She realized she was utterly lost when she got a few feet into the main hall. Nobody was around so she could ask for directions, and the corridor split into different paths. Quiet as a ghost, Simba slipped next to her and asked, 'Need help?'

Pooja jumped, startled, and nodded. They took a path and climbed up the spiral staircase for what seemed like forever. They finally reached the fifteenth floor, which was divided into six sections, three on either side. The doors had the recipients' names, making it easier to find room 1503, Mahi and Ahan's room. Pooja knocked thrice with the bronze knocker hanging carelessly on the door, which swung open to reveal an annoyed Ahan, "Look, man, I don't need con... Oh, Pooja! What brings you here?"

"The memories, I guess," Pooja replied, noticing the strained smile on Ahan's face.

"Of course, come inside, we were just talking about that," he said, swinging the door open completely.

Unlike her room, this one was painted in pastel colors and was furnished with a couch, TV, two desks, a cupboard, and a bed on which Mahi sat, cradling their baby in her arms. She smiled widely at Pooja, put a finger to her lips, and pointed at the baby.

"Is that baby Laila?" Pooja whispered in awe, looking at the cute girl curled up in her mother's arms.

"Yes," she said, before placing her on the bed next to her. She waved her hand, and a layer of black mist formed over her. "To keep her from waking," Mahi clarified.

She sat forward, closer to Pooja, who pulled a chair from one of the desks and plopped opposite her. Ahan heaved a sigh and sat next to Mahi, burying his head on her shoulder in exhaustion.

"Stop overreacting," chided Mahi.

"I am not overreacting! Pooja and I are cousins; this is not okay. It is weird, complicated, and all my life I was trained to hate her and her family. I hate her family, of course, for taking her away from us, but I love *her*!" he exclaimed.

"Cousins?" Pooja's head reeled in shock; she grabbed the chair's handle to steady herself. "What do you mean?"

"You don't remember the memory wheremoment when I discovered that I'm related to you from the book of ancient families?" Ahan mumbled sadly.

She felt at home with Ahan and Mahi, so she said casually, "But if it was *you* who read the book, why would *I* remember it?"

"Huh, that makes sense," Ahan frowned. "Anyway, I'm your cousin. Your grandfather's sister was my grandmother. You don't know this because your grandfather disowned her when she married a man he didn't like."

"Sounds like my grandfather," Pooja shrugged. "Why am I hearing about this only now?"

"That extremely hurt my grandmother and her husband, and we were warned to stay away from you guys because, to be honest, your dad is also kind of like your grandad. We didn't even try to contact you people. Y'all kinda toxic."

"I'm nothing like either of them, though," Pooja quickly clarified, hating how it sounded like a question. How it sounded like she needed reassurance. She *did*, but it was still embarrassing.

"We know that, Pooja," Mahi smiled gently at her and glared at her husband, "But *someone* had to be reminded of that,"

"Guilty," Ahan hung his head like a boy caught stealing chocolates.

"That's fine, your first impression of me is better than my first impression of you," Pooja admitted.

"What was your first impression?"

"Ma'am showed us a picture of both of you, and I thought 'Dude didn't evolve or what? Still looks like an ape from prehistoric times.'"

"Offence," Ahan gasped, placing a hand on his chest in mock horror that sent everyone into peals of laughter.

"Hey, who did you think came when I knocked on the door?" Pooja asked, laughing.

They spent the whole evening and deep into the night hanging out and listening to embarrassing baby stories of Ahan and, unfortunately, her. After having a quick dinner in their room, she bid them goodbye and left. Only after she reached her room did she notice the absence of Simba.

"Simba!" she cried, looking around for him in panic.

'Chill,' his voice resonated in her head, 'I am not your pet. I will come to you when you call me or need guidance. Let me be at peace with my ambush.'

"I did call you now, though," Pooja grinned as if she were drunk. "Why aren't you here? Bad boy, Simba."

She could practically hear Simba's growl of annoyance as her head went silent. She removed her shoes and chucked them in the corner because the room looked too clean. She blasted Taylor Swift's songs as she got ready for bed.

THE DOWNSIDE OF SCHOOL

The next few weeks, quite contrary to the previous days, were torture. It started off with Pooja being stripped of her big room benefits and having to share a room that size with four other recruits, all three were big, mean, ugly, and triplets. They cold-shouldered Pooja and often stole her blanket until she defeated them all in one-on-one combat practice. The first week of the exams consisted of getting to know everyone and a brief school history, which Indra had explained more interestingly. Next, they all got their schedules to complete their tests and were left to prepare themselves.

By the test week, everyone was high on adrenaline; all recruits had to attempt most of their exams in front of an audience. Pooja rolled her eyes every time she thought about it.

Monday arrived, and with it, the first exam: an IQ test. Everyone was called by their role number, which was assigned to them in the order of the date recruited. There was an obstacle course that you had to solve using only your brains. It was conducted in the huge grounds of the palace, the stands full of eager parents, teachers, and the acting king and queen.

Tuesday came, and with it, another obstacle course. This one was more challenging. You had to solve a treasure hunt before a bomb exploded with a person whispering negative thoughts into your ear. Since no rules were mentioned,

Pooja knocked the poor man out to reduce the stress and accidentally found the treasure when she tripped and face-planted straight into it.

Wednesday, with instincts, when you had to play a guessing game. After a while, Pooja realized there was a pattern in the answers and told the examiner. She was threatened with disqualification but later that night, he gave her an apology speech. Pooja could not have been more embarrassed.

Thursday's exam was the easiest. Each contestant was put in a forest near the campus for a whole day. With her experience with recent events and the fact that outdoor woods were her safe haven from her father, Pooja just chilled, making ditches in the floor to prank the other contestants.

Friday's fitness was the hardest for Pooja as her strength was in negatives. She could not lift the bare minimum of weights and struggled to keep up with the rest of the class on the run until one group of teenage guys made a comment about girls being weak. Pooja chased them all across the whole court thrice. The coach lost his voice, blowing the whistle and screaming at her to stop. Letting off steam and exhausting herself like this helped her sleep at night.

Saturday and Sunday were supposed to be rest days, but Pooja was woken up early on Saturday to talk to Indra.

She sat in the chair she had sat in two weeks ago, waiting for His Highness to arrive. When he did, she got down on one knee, head bent low to the ground, with her right fist pressed to her heart, a form of showing utmost respect. She had learned it when she saw a coach doing it and realized that if she was to blend in, she had to treat the king like a king.

"Get up," Indra ordered, seating himself opposite her. "I have been observing your progress throughout the week. I see you have been using your head a lot. You made the bomb exercise, something ninety percent of people struggle with, look like a joke. The trainee, Jayesh, is alright but will carry a black eye for at least a week. The ditches in the forest were a great idea; we also dug them. You did not step on any as you swung from tree to tree. May I ask why?"

"It seemed fun," Pooja shrugged.

"Your luck is outstanding," Indra raised an eyebrow.

"Are we here to talk about that?" Pooja mirrored his expression.

"No, of course not. Mr Singh told me to inform you that he and his wife are no longer going to be recruiters, as Prajwal is out there, trying to get to them. For their and Laila's safety, they have moved back and they will be teachers here," he smiled.

"That's great, yeah, we talked about that, actually. It has been a long time; can I go meet them?" She made puppy eyes.

"Yes, you can, but only after the exam periods are over. We don't want anyone to think that we are biased toward you," he reminded her.

"I have a doubt about the sorting thing." Pooja began.

"Yeah?"

"I'm not sure what to do exactly; Arjun and Avi were vague with their instructions."

Blessings by the BVMs or their wives were only to be given to the Supreme Blessed or the BVM reincarnates, as everyone believed. As Parvati couldn't expose her, she had to choose a minor power of the goddess. Pooja opted for death magic because it was a minor part of the Mahadevi's powers, which she thought was unfair, seeing many opportunities to use that power, and also, Mahi was the house's head. She wasn't sure how to choose.

"Once you are a king, you can communicate with the god who blessed you, if desired," Indra said. "Thus, I spoke to Devendra."

"Hold on, you were Blessed by Indra?" Pooja began to giggle.

Indra waited until she stopped before continuing, "Anyways, before my children's sorting, he told me that the gods would make an exception for the three of you. You must ask for permission from the god you choose to enter his or her house. Good luck."

"That's it?" Pooja blinked.

"Yeah, now go rest before tomorrow's sorting." With that, he dismissed her.

The sorting ceremony reminded her of Harry Potter, but unlike the Sorting Hat, the people being sorted had to walk near the idols of all the gods and stay until one of them glows. When Pooja's turn came, she stared at Lord Yama. Indra told her to ask for permission, but she did not know what exactly to say; she just stared at the statue. She focused on what she wanted to say, repeating 'Please give me permission to enter your house,' and imagined the words flowing from her head into the statue of Lord Yama. As soon as she finished imagining the last brainwave entering the statue, it began to glow. Not believing her luck, she went to the Yama table, shook hands with Mahi and sat next to a girl.

She looked across the table to see a really pretty one staring at her. Her curls were left to fly around, emphasizing her slightly plump face. She looked innocent, but her assessing doe eyes showed her soaking in her surroundings.

"Hello," she greeted.

"Hey," Pooja replied.

"So, what do you think about the gods? It's so cool to be blessed by them, right?" she smiled.

"I guess," Pooja uncertainly tugged at the front of her shirt.

"You aren't satisfied with Yama's blessing?" the girl laughed incredulously.

"It is not like that; I just have a lot on my mind right now."

"Yeah, I get you. I miss my parents a lot. Believe me, it never gets easier."

"That's not the problem at all. I'm happy to be here. This place is awesome, but I'm just gonna need some time to settle down, you know?"

The girl smiled, "Yeah, I guess. I felt that way too. I'm Meher Pillai, by the way."

"I am Pooja Bahl," she extended her hand, turning sideways as Meher did the same. Meher took her hand and shook it.

"So, are you happy with Ganesh's blessing?" Pooja asked, indicating the flag with an elephant's head as its emblem.

"Yeah," she smiled. "I love getting information; honestly, this is the best thing that has happened to me. Both my parents were also Ganesh's, and they really want me to excel and keep up the family name."

"I love that you are making friends, but I really need you to concentrate on what our Majesty is saying, Bahl," a voice said softly.

Pooja turned her head back to see Mahi standing beside her, peering down at them. She gave her one of her most ridiculous smiles and said, "Of course, ma'am."

"It is Mrs. Singh now," she said, unable to suppress the smile forming on her face. Pooja grinned; she loved making Mahi happy. She was the only adult who knew about her father's drinking problem. Mahi had helped Pooja a lot by recommending therapists and, most importantly, making her feel important. Pooja felt the need to repay her all the time, and making her happy was one way of doing so. Even if she didn't appreciate Mahi's way of dealing with things, she believed that, at some point, Mahi truly cared for her. She had to believe that.

Indra stepped onto the stage clad in a long black robe that made him look like a good-looking Severus Snape. He smiled warmly at the whole audience as though pleased by their presence, and Pooja felt herself smiling back. "Look at all of you gathered here. The future, the people we depend on. It is a huge responsibility, but I am confident that every single one of you is capable of that and much more."

He explained how everyone who joined would be in the same dormitories, and all genders would be separate. Each of them would receive their results shortly, the term begins in two weeks, and the curfew is at nine pm. They have to collect their uniforms from their head teacher and should not misuse their powers for pranking. Pooja felt him looking right at her when he said it; she looked back defiantly as though she was not thinking about summoning skeletal hands from the ground to trip people randomly.

The speech ended with all of them filing out into another huge room where hundreds of older students were sitting, laughing, talking, and occasionally throwing bits of food at each other.

"Pooja!" she heard Arjun yell from a table nearest to the exit. It had a huge blue banner with a peacock and a spear – Karthikeya, the God of War.

"Am I allowed to sit here?" she asked, sitting beside him.

"Not every time. Today is free, you can sit wherever you want." He eyed her uniform, "Yama?"

She nodded and reached out for potato fry, which she heaped onto her plate. Arjun was sitting with a couple of other kids; they were obviously his close friends and the popular batch. They were looking at her with interest, the same look every teenager in power has.

"Hi, my name is Pooja," she said.

"Obviously," a girl replied, looking at her as if she were a cockroach. "I am Naina, by the way. Arjun's girlfriend," she reached out to hold Arjun's hand, but Arjun moved it away uncomfortably.

"Yeah," he shrugged. "Nothing serious, though."

Pooja decided that laughing was inappropriate in this situation, so she kept her mouth shut. By the end of the dinner, everyone else warmed up to her a bit, even though she did not like them much. They were all guys and part of a sports team. The sport was called Air Fencing, which was basically fencing but on flying horses. Avi was sitting a few tables apart, at the Ganesh table, talking animatedly with a group of girls who were busy staring, enchanted, at his face.

"Avi has a way with girls," Arjun muttered, chuckling. Pooja smiled sleepily. After a stomach full of food, she only wanted to sink into her bed in the Yama dorms.

"I am going to bed, see you tomorrow," she said and left. Pooja found it incredibly difficult to navigate the castle and found herself in a part of the castle she had never seen before. She moved deeper into the corridor and saw the wall cracked open slightly. She went to it and touched it, realizing that it was a door. She was about to push it open when she heard someone softly panting behind her. She froze and slowly slipped her hand into her pocket where a knife was hidden - part of the uniform - and turned around to see who was stalking her. It was Naina. She immediately dropped her guard.

"Good to see you. Can you please tell me where to go to reach the dorms?"

"Absolutely," she said, coming closer. Suddenly, she pushed Pooja to the door and held her arms. "If I see you with Arjun again, I will end you," she hissed.

"Are you crazy? Let me go!" Pooja gasped and pushed back to try to break free from her clutch; instead, the door behind her flung open. Pooja lost her balance and fell back with Naina right on her. The door automatically slammed shut, leaving them in the dark.

"Shit," Pooja cursed. "Do you have a torch?"

"No," admitted Naina, before she started to glow, "I have fire powers, though, I'm an Agni."

Pooja nodded and looked around. They seemed to be in an abandoned room, with some chunks of the wall broken. It looked like a bomb had gone off in here. Before investigating further, Naina said, "We should get out of here."

"You think?" Pooja asked, turning her attention back to the door which, unfortunately, had no handles.

"How are we going to get out?" Naina asked.

"You have been here longer, you tell me."

"I have never been here before."

"Great, you are so much help," Pooja said sarcastically.

"Shut up," she snapped.

"If only you had not been so jealous, we would not be here," Pooja said, matter-of-factly.

"I was going to let you go! You should not have tried to be so smart there, Brainiac!" Naina exclaimed, furiously making grabbing motions.

"I cannot believe... You know what, no use squabbling. Simba!"

"What?" Naina asked, looking around.

"I am calling my animal guide."

"You named your animal guide?"

"I mean, yeah. Everyone does that, right?"

"No, and how can you access it whenever you like?"

"Maybe spoiled brats don't get to access their guides, or maybe yours just doesn't like you."

"My guide shows up when I need it the most," Naina crossed her arms and muttered.

"Stop calling your guide 'it' and see it as a living being, and maybe it will respond to you," Pooja glowered at her.

'Pooja?' Simba's voice asked in her head.

"Simba, where are you?"

'I am outside this wall. Why did you go in?'

"Long story, get help!"

She heard no reply, so she assumed that he had left to get help. She sank down, her back facing the door. A gut feeling told her she should get out of here as quickly as possible. Naina sat close to her; she looked pretty in her uniform. The white shirt tucked neatly into her skirt with the leggings made her look like she came straight from a K-drama with her brown doe eyes and soft, full lips. Her boots were neatly polished, unlike Pooja's, which already had a clear layer of dirt on them. She suddenly realized she was feeling drowsy; Naina's head was also drooping. She slapped her face as it was the only way to keep herself from sleeping.

There were other ways, but this was the most satisfactory.

"What the hell?" she exclaimed.

"No sleeping until we are rescued," Pooja sharply commanded her.

They both waited, trying not to doze off for a couple of minutes when they heard footsteps echoing from outside. They slowly rose to their feet and began banging on the door.

"Here!" Pooja yelled. Suddenly, she felt time slow down, the air thickening in danger. She could hear each vibration as Naina banged the door. The same laughter she heard in the last memory echoed through the chamber, or was it only in her head? She grabbed Naina's arm and pulled her down hard. She fell with a soft 'thump' next to Pooja. The feeling stopped as suddenly as it started.

"Stay back, kids," Indra's voice came through the other side of the door. Both girls scrambled back as the door slammed open again. They both rushed outside, expecting sympathy, but seeing a furious Indra. "Explain," he said, his voice as cold as ice.

POV YOUR FAVORITE TEACHER IS ABSENT

After explaining what happened in the King's Chamber, Indra told them to be careful, gave them a bottle of water, and sent them to their dormitories with directions. Pooja wanted to collapse onto her bunk and never wake up, but was interrupted by Meher.

"Hey, where were you?" she whispered, blocking the entrance to the Yama dorms.

"Got lost but I am here now," Pooja murmured sleepily.

Obviously not getting the hint, Meher began, "We got our timetables. Mrs. Singh gave me yours when you were gone. She asked about you, actually."

"Oh?" Pooja was instantly alert when Mahi's name was mentioned.

"She wanted to know how your dinner was. And the squabble with Naina," Meher smirked.

"How did she know?" Pooja asked incredulously.

"It was pretty obvious she was jealous," Meher tilted her head slightly, widening her eyes.

"Why?" Pooja frowned, the sleep entering her system again.

"Arjun talks about you a lot. He kept complimenting your performance in the tests and comparing it with

Naina's, maybe that is why she hates you," Meher suggested with a shrug.

Pooja was no expert on relationships, but she guessed this was bad boyfriend behavior, so she asked a much simpler question: "How do you know this?"

"I was eavesdropping, duh!" Meher said, slipping a piece of paper wrapped in hard, plastic-like see-through material. Looking at it, Pooja saw it was a timetable. She glanced at their first period tomorrow: History. She stifled a groan and bid Meher a good night. She crept into her dorm, where her roommates were already asleep.

The dorm itself was huge, separated year-wise, with the new joiners closest to the door. As the recruits usually had minor powers, Pooja was sharing her bed space with a bunch of six-year-olds. She tried not to cringe at that, but at least due to her performance in her tests, she didn't have to attend *all* her classes with them. Only power training, Sanskrit, and, embarrassingly, fitness. A huge chandelier at the centre of the ceiling stretched across the whole space like a spiderweb. It mimicked the effect of moonlight that soothed her. Pooja shoved her timetable into a bag that was made for her and placed it neatly next to her bed.

She barely got into a pair of pajamas folded tidily into a small wardrobe next to her bed before sinking into her fluffy bed. The sheets, pillows, and quilt were a deep midnight color. She drifted into an uneasy sleep.

Prajwal stared down at her, his eyes red and burning. "Come find me," Pooja couldn't move or say anything. He turned and moved toward two figures—a lean, tall brunette with terrified brown eyes and an athletic one with startling blue eyes and choppy hair—Anaaya and Thalia. He took a knife and ran it across a whetstone, which sparked at every point of contact. He turned back to give her a cold, sharp smile.

He raised the knife and began his work on the two of them. Pooja could only scream in her head, begging him to stop. She watched as Prajwal carved the two most important people to her. Covered in their blood, he crouched next to her. He slowly licked the blood off one finger. "You want revenge? Come and get it."

Pooja woke up, filling her lungs with air. "Just a nightmare," she told herself, but her heart wouldn't stop racing. The dream felt too real. She could not bear it anymore. Checking that everyone was fast asleep, she tiptoed quietly to the dorm door and snuck out. She stuck to the shadows, avoiding the night guards patrolling the corridors, and went outside.

She began to walk toward the beach and saw stairs leading inside the dividing wall. She climbed up to the very top, where the wall smoothed out, and sat down, swinging her legs on the other side. She closed her eyes, letting the fresh air and sea breeze take away all the negative thoughts from her head. She smiled the first genuine smile she had smiled in a very long time, thinking about her friends.

"You look beautiful when you do that, you should do it more often," a voice whispered softly. Pooja's eyes sprang open as she turned her head quickly to see who had interrupted her moment of peace. It was Avi. His hair danced to the rhythm of the air, his eyes shining as he assessed her, his lips stretched into a wide, carefree smile.

"Maybe I need a reason to smile more often," she replied. "What are you doing here?"

"I could ask you the same," he said as he approached her. "Not thinking of jumping off, are you?"

"No," Pooja startled.

"Good, because the air around us is bewitched, it will throw your ass right back on the wall," he grinned.

"Seriously?" Pooja drawled.

"Oh yeah," he quirked an eyebrow before launching himself to the side. True enough, he seemed to fly back and fall on his buttocks magically. "Ouch."

Pooja laughed, "Don't tell me you're here to attempt suicide."

"No, of course not. This is my getaway from the world. My peaceful place, if you would like to call it," he sat beside her, wincing slightly.

"I was here for the same reason," Pooja looked away as his honey-brown eyes met her dull ones.

"Then it can be *our* peace place," Avi turned his head to look at her. She felt a slight blush on her face, probably because of the wind. "The gods know this wall is big enough for both of us. And an army."

Pooja laughed again, her teeth chattering slightly. "It is kinda cold," she said, rubbing her arms.

"You should have brought a jacket; too bad you did not," he said, pulling his jacket closer for warmth. Huffing, Pooja tugged the jacket off his right shoulder and wrapped it around herself. She put her right hand into the sleeve and snuggled closer to Avi.

"You could have been kind and offered," she mumbled against his shoulder, which she was crushed into. Avi laughed his beautiful laugh again, which sounded like a bird, filled with joy. He said nothing as he rested his head on hers. They stayed like that, watching wave after wave crash into the sandy beach, until Avi asked her, "What brings you here, anyway?"

Pooja considered the question for a minute and readjusted her face so her cheek was pressed against his shoulder, not her nose. She felt a bond with Avi, something she never felt before. Maybe because he did not freak her out by being weirdly distant and snobby like Arjun when he was with Naina and his popular friends. Maybe because he did not judge her or threaten to report her for breaking the curfew like so many others would probably have. Maybe because his presence calmed her like Thalia and Anaaya, but she trusted him. She told him everything about the room, Prajwal, and her concerns except the dream. It was too raw and fresh for her to discuss it with a near stranger.

After a long, hard pause, she said, "I am going to investigate this room. I will find out what it is and how it is used so I can know what Prajwal did. He seemed scared and was begging for help. If I find it out, I can help defeat Prajwal. I have a powerful feeling." The gods knew how badly she wanted to defeat him.

"Absolutely not," Avi said firmly. Pooja's heart sank; she expected everyone's refusal for her crazy ideas, but Avi's rejection stung deeper because he was the first person she trusted in that place, and now... "*We* will be investigating," Pooja looked up in surprise to see determination in Avi's eyes. "You are not alone; you never will be. I am not going to desert you or snitch on you. We are doing this together, whether you like it or not."

Pooja smiled widely, "Maybe *you* will give me a reason to smile."

The next morning, Pooja woke up in her bed, reliving her night once more. She loved the friendship she shared with Avi already. She got dressed and went to breakfast, once more sitting behind Meher, so they could talk as they weren't allowed to sit with each other.

"Hey," she chirped, the lack of sleep not bothering her for once.

Meher looked up and smirked, "Where were you last night?"

"What do you mean?" Pooja feigned ignorance as she served herself some chutney and bondas.

"What I mean is, did you sneak out with Arjun?"

"No, Avi. I mean, it was not planned, exactly," Pooja told Meher about everything that happened, including Prajwal.

"Wait, no way. If you want answers, you should go to the Majesty. I mean, if it is about Prajwal, it is serious."

"Avi did not think that."

"He probably agreed with you because he wanted you to like him."

"Wait, are you saying he was *flirting* with me?" Pooja asked, suddenly laughing. She found that she could not stop; she doubled over and laughed until she could not breathe. When she looked up, Meher gave her a look of disdain that looked hilarious, and she burst into laughter once again.

"Or," Meher said, annoyed, over the sound of her laughter. "He must have had a family tiff with his uncle."

This stopped her. "Uncle?"

"Yeah. Avi and Arjun are the Majesty's nephews. Why do you think they look alike?" Meher rolled her eyes as though it was obvious.

'Maybe because they are father and sons,' Pooja thought but did not say out loud. She 'oooooohhh'ed and nodded as though this made perfect sense, widening her eyes.

"Wait, how did you know?"

"All the girls' quarters are in the same dormitory, year-wise. I heard you sneaking out as I was coming from the restroom."

After a quick breakfast, she and Meher left for the castle, where classes were taken, called the Education Centre. They climbed three flights of spiral stairs to reach the history classroom that had 'HISTORY' stamped on the door in bold. All the houses took classes together based on their skill levels in particular subjects. Meher and she shared most of their classes, which greatly helped her since she couldn't make many friends fast. They were a couple of minutes early so they decided to explore the hallway, with lots of convincing on Pooja's part.

Pooja looked around and saw three doors. She pushed open the first one to look, while Meher insisted that she not. The room contained many weapons, all of them too old to be used. They had labels and dates dating as far back as the Mahabharata times. They had all kinds of artillery, ranging from bows to javelins, and even a few instruments that looked like torture devices. The room had a slight tinge of rust and dirt from the weapons. The lighting dimmed as the room stretched far, and Meher was terrified. Pooja shut the door and moved on.

The second door had different clothes that Pooja recognized as clothing styles from centuries ago. Most of them were handmade, and the intricate designs were clearly visible. The clothes portrayed the fashion of people from all sectors of society, neatly labelled in Sanskrit and English. Somehow, the atmosphere was enchanted to smell and feel like fabric and paint.

The third door, however, opened her into a whole new world. There were mud houses and straw houses built symmetrically and in order along a mud road. The aromatic smells of sweets wafted through the air, making Pooja crave some *motichoor laddoos*. She realized that it was a room made to depict a time in the past. The dirt roads spread like veins across the floor with a few houses having personal gardens. Pooja squinted to see a few agricultural fields that looked like the farmers had left quickly. The entire place seemed sad and empty. She wondered which place this was.

Impressed with the school's budget, she went back to the main room, checking her watch that her parents had given her. It was 8:58, two minutes before History. She nodded to Meher and pushed open the door, ready to see Mahi again.

However, a man she had never seen before stood behind the teacher's desk. He had sandy brown and gray hair, almost shaved off. He had no facial hair, but wrinkles around his eyes, making him look ancient when he could not have been more than forty. Before she could speak, a sense of déjà vu disabled her ability to utter a single word. Just two feet away from her was the first time she had met Mahi, Ahan, and Prajwal. She remembered the day clearly in full detail. She was pulled back into reality by the new professor.

"Hello, welcome to my class," he smiled at them. "You're early."

"Hi, sir," Meher said, reaching out to shake his extended hand.

"Where is Mahi Ma'am, I mean Mrs Singh?" Pooja blurted out, rudely ignoring the hand.

The smile waned on the professor's face. "You must be Miss Bahl. She wanted me to tell you that she could not make it today. I will be taking the class instead."

"Why?" she demanded.

"I don't know, please settle down, Miss Bahl."

"Is she okay?" she asked.

"Yes," the man said, clearly losing his patience. Meher grabbed Pooja's hand and led her to the farthest corner of the classroom.

"You don't need to get on his bad side on the very first day, Pooja. You don't even know his name," she whispered softly, pulling out her history textbook, a blank spiral-bound notebook, and a pencil box all assigned to her by the school. Pooja pulled out her own stuff, without a word, agreeing with her. Getting on his bad side will not help; she has to figure it out on her own.

As soon as the bell rang, twenty other students filed in, filling up the classroom. As soon as the chattering stopped, the man walked up to the centre of the room and turned to the board.

"My name is Ravi Kumar," he scrawled in cursive, "I was fortunate to be blessed by Agnidev, and I will be your history teacher until further notice."

"Excuse me, Mr Kumar," the guy sitting next to her said, his hand shooting up.

"Yes, Mr…"

"Gupta, sir. According to the list, our teacher is supposed to be Mahi Singh."

Pooja frowned. "Where did he find that?"

"Behind your timetable, there is a list of all the teachers who will take our classes, did you not notice it?" Meher whispered back.

"Yes," Ravi said, "but she is not well now, so I will be substituting. Any more questions?" He looked around the still, quiet classroom. "Okay, now we will begin with our lesson. Turn to page one of your textbooks. Chapter One: Introduction to Our Past."

The lesson ended quickly enough, after that they had Chemistry with Anita Senha, Geography with Manoj Singh, and Forest Skills with Sumita Arora. After lunch, they had combat practice with multiple teachers, where Pooja learnt she could shoot a bow as well as fight with dual swords. The teacher called her the best student in the class and gave her a gold star, much to her embarrassment and the delight of the six-year-olds surrounding her. The few older ones included the triplets who bullied her, so she didn't bother to be associated with their group. Then, their gym coach, Mukesh Bhardwaj, informed them that from next week, they would have fitness classes from 5-6 am every morning and encouraged all the little ones to wake up early. He just stared at Pooja, who was heating up in embarrassment for being the only one who *wasn't* six in his class.

Finally, the school bell sounded again, signaling the end of the day. Pooja gathered her things and met Meher in the locker room. They began to head to their dorms, discussing the day's events.

"Vinay Gupta is the most annoying person I have seen to date, and that is saying something," Pooja chuckled and looked up to see Avi casually standing there, noticing her; he gave a half-smile.

"I will leave you here," Meher said, walking inside.

"Hey," Avi said.

"Hey yourself. What brings you here?" Pooja asked.

"About last night. I thought we could use some help, so I told the one person I could trust in this place," Avi said, shrugging. Arjun emerged from behind the pillar, his bag hung carelessly over one shoulder. He seemed to have rushed there.

"Sorry, I am late. I got held up," he said.

"Teachers or Naina?" Avi asked with a teasing smile.

"Teachers," Arjun clarified, turning to Pooja, he said, "If you are thinking about asking my dad about the room, he is not going to tell you a thing. I decided to eavesdrop on whatever was going on this morning after Avi told me what happened. They have Mrs Singh held up; they were interrogating her. Apparently Prajwal used to roam around in that corridor frequently, occasionally taking you there. They all are in the dark about why he took you there, and they don't want you to find out. Everyone is going to pretend that place is not related to Prajwal and tell you that your theory is wrong and you're overanalyzing things because of stress and pressure."

"Whoa, Arjun, you have been resourceful," Pooja marvelled. "I was not thinking about that, but what do we do then?"

"Well, we use the library. There are many books on the castle there, its insides, outsides, and all."

The three went up to the library in the Education Centre and began to read the books one by one until dinnertime. This became a routine for them: going to the library whenever they were free and trying to find out about the castle. Pooja learnt that the castle was not located in Hyderabad at all; in fact, at irregular intervals, the castle changes places, which nobody would notice until they left the place. The castle was a whole city with places for people to live. This whole place would be replaced by barren land when the castle moved. It was a defense mechanism installed in the Mughal times to make it harder to invade the castle, but there was no mention of the room they found.

"It has been over three months since you went to the secret room," Arjun said. "And you still have not heard from Mahi?"

"No," Pooja said, biting into her wrap, "I am not even allowed in the teacher's quarters anymore."

Pooja, Arjun, and Avi were sitting on the wall, observing the sunset, and taking a break from the vigorous studies they had to do for their half-yearly exams, which would begin in around a month's time. Pooja had not heard from Ahan, Mahi or Indra for a long time and she was beyond worried. She tried to distract herself by searching for the room, but that brought no good news either. She was in the dark about so many things, not in control, like Thalia's death... no. She could not afford to think about that either.

"It is going to be fine," Avi softly assured her. "She will not be hurt."

"I know, it would just be nice to do something useful for once," Pooja said, flinging her empty aluminum wrapper into the air, which was immediately disintegrated by a gust of wind... a cleaning technique of the castle.

"It is obvious that the three of us have had no luck finding out about the room. We are down to three books, and I am in the last chapter of mine," Arjun stated.

"Me too!" Avi and Pooja exclaimed, disheartened.

"We need more help. Who can we trust, though?" Arjun asked in a resigned voice.

"Um, how about Meher?" Pooja suggested.

"Who is Meher?" Arjun asked, confused.

"Oh, right. You both have not met officially yet. She is the girl I roam with all the time."

"Oh, her? I know her. If you trust her, I trust her," Arjun said, making Pooja smile.

"I will go ask her," Pooja stood up and left for Meher's dormitory. Avi and Arjun were amazing people. Although she had not trusted Arjun for a long time, she realized he was just a kid trying to be perfect for his parents—something she could relate to.

Meher was, as usual, curled up in her bed, revising.

"Hey," Pooja called, standing near the door.

"What?" Meher snapped, not even looking up.

"I have to tell you something important; it is urgent. Let's go for a walk," Pooja said seriously enough to make Meher look up.

She shrugged, put the book down and said, "Okay."

Pooja took her to the ground, away from the training centre , past the wall, onto the beach. There was a lighthouse in the farthest corner where they sat down. Pooja told her everything from the start: her obsession with the room, her guesses about how the room is important, how Indra had Mahi, bringing outraged gasps from Meher. For what seemed like hours, Meher remained silent. Pooja could hear her heartbeat in the silence of the evening, thumping in a regular pattern.

Finally, Meher said, "I wish you had come to me before."

"I know," Pooja interrupted, "I just did not want to get you into trouble."

"Pooja! Don't interrupt. I am not being emotional. I am just saying, you wasted your time. I have the book that mentions the secret room."

"What?!" Pooja exclaimed incredulously.

"Yeah. The day you told me about the room, I knew you would search for it. I went to the library, got the thickest book I could find about the castle, and have been reading it since."

"Why did you wait so long to tell me?"

"That is because I found it today. I was waiting for you to get back so I could surprise you with it."

"You are a genius!" Pooja laughed and threw her arms around Meher. She had solved one of her problems; now, she could solve the next. Meher disentangled herself from Pooja, smiling softly. Pooja dropped Meher near the dorms and left her to call Arjun and Avi.

She went up to Arjun's dorm in the Karthikeya block and knocked on the door. It was flung open by a guy who could not have been more than nine. He was chubby in a cute way with dark hair and blue eyes. He smiled and waved her in. The boy, Rushi, was one of the sweetest nine-year-olds who could knock you out easily. Pooja liked him a lot; he was like the younger brother she never had. Pooja went up to Arjun's bed to see him and Avi, going through their books.

"Guys, Meher has what we need," she whispered excitedly. It was enough to get them going, and within ten minutes all of them were on the wall, flipping through the pages in the book.

Meher was not kidding about its thickness. It was 2 feet long and wide, black in color, with its writing in gold, in Sanskrit. It said: Secrets Unveiled. It had over 20,000 pages, and the room was on page 18,896. Pooja found the page, which was in English, and read it out loud.

"The Death Room, also known as The Ancestral Resting Place, is a dangerous room," she looked up. "Such a lively beginning."

Avi let out a nervous chuckle, which Pooja mirrored.

"In this room, you can do anything from communicating with the memories of your ancestors to summoning them and giving them another chance at surviving in this world."

"How could someone do that? Who would have that much power?" Avi asked.

"Would you shut up and let her continue? It's important," Meher snapped.

"If it was so important, why didn't you come to us?" Avi snapped back.

"Just was waiting until you knuckleheads decided to come to me," Meher shrugged as Avi snarled in her face. "Guys, stop," Arjun intervened. "Pooja, go on."

Pooja swallowed a lump in her throat and continued, "This can only be done by a powerful descendant, likely the Prince or Princess. Others would succumb to the room's power and face a fate worse than death. This room can also be used to prevent your death. This can be done by sacrificing people your ancestors hate and chanting the correct mantras. If done wrong, the room will collapse, killing you and releasing the spirits contained forever."

Pooja's heart felt like it was being squeezed. The dread was so heavy, it hurt her. Prajwal could've used the room to be immortal. He could've done so many things in that room, and she probably had something to do with it, too. What if every bad thing Prajwal did was possible because of her? The guilt of the possibility that she played a part in any of that killed her. She looked around to see her companions staring at her, stunned. Meher sympathetically looked at her.

"Pretty dark," Avi said, letting out a nervous laugh. "Meher could have told us this long ago."

"Meher found it today," Meher snapped.

Pooja quickly spoke, not wanting a distraction, "Ancestors, huh? I wonder why Prajwal was doing it."

Before they could discuss it further, Pooja spotted Vinay Gupta, the guy from the history class who was recruited at the same time as her, sprinting toward them. She quickly shoved a bookmark to mark the page and put it in Arjun's open bag that they had grabbed before going out.

"Hey, I have been searching for you guys everywhere," Vinay gasped as he reached them.

"What's up, bro?" Arjun asked. Pooja doubted he had ever talked to him before.

"What's up is that the Majesty is calling Pooja, you, and Avi to his office right now," he leaned closer to them, his eyes sparkling in excitement. "Guys, I think you are about to be assigned a mission!"

Missions were a big thing; they were tasks that were completed by people deemed worthy enough to do them. This was an honorable thing that, if completed successfully, would give you badges of honor and extra dessert privileges. Being chosen for a mission three months into your training was rare. This usually happened when a war loomed over them or they wanted the people to stay away from the castle. Pooja assumed it was both in their case. Nonetheless, they could not openly defy the king's summons, so they left after entrusting Meher with Arjun's bag.

Pooja felt chills running up her spine as they entered the familiar elevator. Missions usually ended badly with lots of death, and she could not find out why Indra would send them on a task like this. Almost as though he could read her mind, Arjun leaned over and whispered, "In case you were wondering, these missions will just prove to everyone that we are capable and trustworthy enough to rule over them."

Pooja could not help but notice his breath smelled like mint, fanning her face as he spoke, calming her down. She fought down the blood rushing to her cheeks at their close contact, glad that the lift doors parted open. All three of them stepped out and knocked.

Once again, the door swung open like magic. The three of them went inside, mechanically bowed, and sat in the chairs facing the king. Upon seeing them, he nodded.

"I have picked wisely," he said in a rich tone, handing over scrolls to each of them.

"These scrolls contain the details of the mission you three have been entrusted to go upon," a man spoke in a thick South Indian accent on the king's right. "I am Jai Yennamuri, the Majesty's right hand man and most trusted minister," he stated, pointedly looking at the inquiring look on Pooja's face.

'Not close enough to know our real identities,' Pooja thought. She broke open the kingdom's seal and unrolled the scroll:

Miss Pooja Bahl, Yama Dharma Raj's Chosen, Controller of Death,

You have been entrusted, with your mission mates, to retrieve the recently lost Book of our brave ancestors. The Book has been misplaced by soldiers who, unknowingly, put us at risk. The Head of your House will guide you.

The supplies you will require, along with your weapons, will be delivered to you shortly.

Wishing you all the best,

The Royal Highness,

Indra Sharma.

"Mrs Singh will accompany me, Your Highness?" Pooja asked, feeling relieved that she was all right.

"Yes, Mrs Singh and well, Ahan isn't letting his wife go alone, so he too." he turned to Jai, "Yennamuri, if you don't mind, I would like to converse with my nephews and their friend alone."

"I will take my leave, sire," he bowed and left.

"Pooja," Indra rested his chin on his hands. "I am very sorry. I have held your cousin and his wife with me for a long time. You must know that this was for your safety. Prajwal…"

"Save it, please. I know what you were doing. I also know that it was wrong of you to do that. I understand how worried you are about Prajwal, but interrogating them and treating them like it's their fault cannot be right," Pooja retaliated in frustration.

"You are right," Indra sighed. "Any more questions before you guys leave?"

Pooja exchanged glances with Arjun and Avi, silently asking permission. When she got it, she said, "Yes. What have you found out after interrogating them?"

"They had absolutely no idea about anything," Indra sighed.

"Why did you keep them for so long, then?" Pooja raised an eyebrow.

"Pooja, the book of ancestors holds the key to defeating Prajwal. We think that Prajwal may have summoned one of his ancestors through you, and now his ancestor is helping him mobilize his army. That book will tell us who he might have summoned. If we send the ancestor back to hell, the Prajwal problem will be resolved."

"How do you know that Prajwal's ancestor is calling the shots, though? It could be Prajwal himself," Pooja offered a different viewpoint.

"There is no way. Mahi is extremely skilled when it comes to her powers. Her career path was to work as the official Yama representative in my court, but due to her marriage with Ahan, she did not. If Prajwal and Mahi get married, their kids will be incredibly powerful, inheriting both mind control and spirit control. However, Prajwal is married to another woman whom he loves very dearly, according to some of my spies. He seems like a completely different, good man with her. But he disappears into a chamber and comes out like the monster he is made out to be. Our theory is that his ancestor is held in that chamber, and he planned the attack on you guys because Prajwal will not willingly risk his relationship with his wife. In theory."

"Alright, that's all," Pooja said, practically feeling her brain expanding, adapting to store all the new information she had gathered.

Indra led them all to a room next to his chamber, where Ahan and Mahi were waiting. A table was placed in front of them, and backpacks containing all the essential supplies were placed on it. The backpacks changed color and design to blend into the background. They both stopped talking once they noticed Pooja enter.

"Hey bud, how is school life treating you?" Ahan asked with a grin.

"Like shit. I've been exhausting myself for the past three months. How have you been?" Pooja asked, containing her emotions and maintaining the same calm as Ahan.

"We have been busy too, trying to locate the book. We found it; now we have to retrieve it," Ahan informed her.

After thoroughly rechecking their supplies, the trio was given clothes appropriate for a mission and an hour to say their goodbyes. Pooja bid adieu to Avi and Arjun near the Karthikeya dorm and went to hers. She found everyone huddled near the door, eagerly waiting for something or someone.

"Finally, she shows up," Meher grinned. During these months, she was basically an adopted Yama.

"Hey, what's up?" Pooja asked.

"What's up is," their dorm head Aakanksha said, "is that you got a mission and you didn't bother to tell us."

"Vinay told you?" Pooja rolled her eyes. "When I get back, I will murder him. For the record, I just got back from briefing."

"Well, congratulations."

Pooja spent the rest of her free time listening to the advice of some of the Yamas who were part of missions previously. When the time finally arrived for her to leave, Pooja felt extremely nervous. She could only think about the last time she was out in the real world, when her best friend died.

'Who will die now?' a voice inside her head whispered, as Pooja looked at her fellow mission mates. 'Nobody, not if I can help it,' Pooja retorted, then realized she was arguing with herself. She felt Arjun's hand slip into hers as he leaned forward to whisper in her ear, "Are you ready?"

"Nope," Pooja cheerily replied, swinging her arms as she walked toward the van Ahan and Mahi were boarding. It was true, she wasn't ready; she was still scared. But she was sure she could do anything as long as her friends were with her.

THE FUN ROAD TRIP
(SPOILER ALERT: IT WASN'T FUN)

Two hours into the mission, Pooja understood that missions were not fun. She, Arjun, Avi, Mahi, and Ahan drove calmly without any disturbance. That was *fine*, but not really *fun*.

"What makes missions so honorable if all we do is collect a package and drive back to the base like a delivery person?" Pooja asked, finally sick of the peace and quiet. "To be entirely honest, history class is more interesting."

"History *is* interesting," Mahi countered from the front. Naturally, she was sitting next to her driving husband.

"Once you begin to work on your powers, your godly aura strengthens as your brain adjusts to develop your skills. The more powerful you are, the greater the aura. This means that you are more prone to attacks from asuras who can sense this aura. Exiting the base itself is dangerous; we should be lucky that we have not been attacked yet," Avi said.

"It has nothing to do with luck, Avi. I have a strong feeling that we are purposefully not being attacked by any asuras because dad can't risk the Prince and the Princess dying," Arjun snorted.

The van screeched to a halt suddenly, throwing Pooja forward. She slammed violently into the seat in front of her.

Ahan turned back, eyes wide. "What do you mean 'Prince and Princess?'"

"We are Indra's sons and, as per the ancient tales, we are supposed to lead the world's people to war against the asuras. Pooja is the Princess; one of us will have the honor of being the Prince," Arjun simply stated.

"I didn't know this. Did you?" Ahan rounded on his wife.

"No, I thought you guys were just normal students. Oh gods, do we bow to you?" Mahi asked, eyes uncertain.

"Don't be ridiculous, ma'am. We have not done anything to earn such respect yet. Arjun and Avi have been sitting protected in the base while I was moping about my daddy issues," Pooja snapped. "I can't believe Indra didn't tell you. He knows how close we are. Honestly, I thought you knew. I'm so sorry."

Ahan and Mahi simultaneously looked at each other, communicating without words. Ahan started the van again, "Don't be sorry. Even after all we did for him, if Indra doesn't trust us, it's his godsdamn fault."

"Ahan," Mahi calmly replied, "I think you know why he didn't tell us. Prajwal knew that Pooja was the Princess, so he took her to the chamber, meaning he did it."

"Did what?" Avi asked.

"Back when we were friends, Prajwal used to have this mad idea. He was talking about how, to clarify things that happened in the past, we could summon our ancestors and question them about it. He wanted to bring a couple of great people back from the dead so they could help us in the final war. Although we discouraged the idea, Prajwal was passionate about it. He was a legend because his great-great-grandfather, Prajwal, was a hero. He died saving Arjun and Avi's great-grandfather, the sole male of the family. If he had not done that, Krishna's blessing wouldn't have happened. Prajwal wanted to get him back because it was rumored that he had the key to defeating the asuras once and for all, but he died before he could share the knowledge." Ahan nodded as he spoke, driving again.

"Yeah, Prajwal was crazy about trying to bring him back to life. He used to spend hours researching how to do it. He found the chamber you went into and showed it to us. Although he couldn't summon his ancestor," Mahi continued.

"He didn't have the powers," Pooja completed. "Wait, Indra said something about how you were extremely skilled and all in Yama's blessings. Didn't he try to use you?"

Mahi looked at Ahan, who seemed extremely unhappy about the current topic of discussion. He stared straight ahead, glaring at the cars in front as if they offended him somehow. She cleared her throat, "Actually, he did. I just didn't know it. Prajwal used to encourage me a lot to pursue my Blessing, all that support led to me developing feelings for him. Much like getting a PhD, we can develop our skills outside classroom learning. We can test the limits and create new methods of using our powers. If we do that, we will be awarded a high position and well-respected because it is tedious. I started pursuing my skills, and I absolutely enjoyed it. I was the one who discovered that Yamas can sense souls; a harmless example is, if a woman is carrying a child, we will be able to see that there are two souls in her body. Similarly, we can tell if a spirit possesses somebody."

"I can do that? That is so cool!" Pooja exclaimed.

"No, you can't do that, Pooja," Arjun corrected. "You need to be super powerful to be able to achieve something like that. You need to use your powers in your daily life; using your powers should be like brushing your teeth for you. Right now, since you barely use them, it will be impossible. After your basic training is complete, you can use some of the harmless aspects of your powers in your daily life; this will give you the ability to do cool stuff like sensing souls without, you know, dying."

"When will the basic training start? I can't wait to finally use my powers. I haven't seen anyone use theirs except for your dad," Pooja sighed wistfully, imagining all the fun things she could do with her powers.

"Wait, your training was supposed to start on the first day of school," Avi sounded astounded. "That is the whole point of the base, to help you control your powers before they control you."

"I think that it's partially my fault. I was supposed to train the new recruits with their powers, but I disappeared on them," Mahi placed her hand on Ahan's and squeezed it slightly. She didn't bother to take it back.

"Not your fault. It's my dad's, blame him and only him," Arjun sighed, sinking back into his seat, closing his eyes. Sitting next to him, Pooja could feel him tense. She placed her hand around his clenched fist.

"You okay?" she asked softly.

"Absolutely not. My dad talks about a fair chance and all, but he rigged everything. *We* were supposed to be working to find the location of the book, not Mr and Mrs Singh. He is giving us everything on a silver platter."

"Why are you complaining?" Avi cried in exasperation.

"Try to understand what I'm going through here!" Arjun fumed.

"Oh, I am *so* sorry that your father is trying to make your life easier. Let me apologize to you that you can take credit and rise to greatness without lifting a finger. Oh, I feel *so* bad that you have *always* been the one dad wants on that throne, and I *sincerely* apologize that getting there is a piece of cake for you," Avi sneered.

"I don't want that throne!" Arjun snapped. "Not like this. I want to earn that thing, and when I am getting crowned, I want to be convinced that I am fully capable of leading this world. I don't want my fate to be decided by a godsdamn glowing bracelet!"

Pooja was taken aback at this sudden outburst. Every time they had talked about them being leaders, Arjun always sounded like he had no doubt he'd be able to live up to the people's expectations. He was the charming twin, the one who did not complain, the polite one, the smart one, the studious one, the brave one, the one as skillful as his namesake in archery, the one who dedicated his life to the throne. Now, it sounded as though he doubted everything he had done.

"Arjun, I don't think you are unworthy," Pooja said, her voice small. "From what I have seen, you are an amazing person and you would make a great leader."

"Thank you," Arjun's voice turned hoarse as if he was holding back tears. "I may be good at leading people in small stuff like hunting trips but I don't think I can be responsible for so many people. I'm terrified."

"It's natural to be scared. You have the capability to improve your leadership skills. Nobody is asking you to ascend the throne now. You've been training your whole life for this. You can play your role and compensate for my lower-than-expected performance," Pooja chuckled dryly.

Arjun smiled softly, small dimples appearing on his face, and covered Pooja's hand with his own. "I seriously doubt that, Princess."

"This is what I am talking about," Avi jeered. "You have everything. I don't get why father pretends that we have an equal chance of ruling. Everybody wants you to rule, even Pooja. Nobody thinks I am capable of anything."

"That is so not true, Avi," Pooja protested, "I *do* think you are capable. The difference between you and Arjun is that you are confident about your abilities but Arjun isn't. You both are equally likely to be the one. What you said about your dad wanting Arjun to rule may or may not be true, but he does not control the fates. His opinion seriously doesn't matter, what matters is what *you* think of yourself."

"Wise words, Pooja. Unfortunately, that's all they are, empty words. You don't mean it; you are just trying to be nice. You want Golden Boy Arjun, don't bother lying to me," Avi turned away and rested his head on the window.

Pooja was hurt by Avi's words; she knew from experience that empty promises and empty words hurt badly. She tried her best not to lie because she was lied to her whole life, and that ruined her completely. Avi knew this very well; it hurt Pooja that he would hurt her like this to win a petty argument.

"Maybe I do prefer him," she hissed back. She heard Avi's quiet, dark chuckle, but she ignored it. She turned away, blinking back the tears that were threatening to fall.

"Hey, I'm sorry he's being so rude to you," Arjun breathed. "For whatever it's worth, I know you meant everything you said. It's nice to have someone like you as a friend, Princess. I know that you will never hurt me or lie to me. I feel safe around you because of your honesty, and that means everything to me. I trust you more than anyone, and I trust you won't break my trust."

Arjun's words stirred up a mixture of emotions in Pooja's heart. She could feel that Arjun wasn't only trying to comfort her but was being truthful. Pooja rarely received any meaningful compliments; Arjun's were too sweet for her. His niceness was a whole new experience, but it made her happy, an emotion that she wasn't used to feeling. She trusted Arjun much more than she probably should but she knew that he wouldn't let her down. The tears rolled down her cheeks as she buried her face into Arjun's shoulder, silently mourning her past life, Thalia, and finally getting rid of the rage and pain she felt by the memories of her parents off her chest.

IT GETS FUN HERE FOR A WHILE

Pooja fell asleep, for the first time in months, peacefully. Her slumber was cut short when Arjun shook her awake.

"What is going on?" Pooja mumbled groggily, yawning.

"Good morning, Sleepyhead, we are here. All we have to do is get the book from a couple of asuras, no biggie," Arjun grinned.

"Yeah. Do you think they will hand it over if we say 'please'?" Pooja asked innocently.

"I really don't think so," Arjun replied with a smile.

"If you two are done chatting, we will talk about our plan of action," Mahi called from the front. She pulled a lever under her seat and turned it 180 degrees so she was facing them, and Ahan copied her. Mahi pulled out a small book and pen from her bag and flipped it open to a blank page.

"Okay, so the book is in a chest, sitting on a table in the centre of the gathering," she drew a chest in the middle of the page. "There are 20 asuras, 5 guarding each corner." She drew stick figures with devil horns. "Our plan is to have someone draw the asuras away from the book while the others take it and leave. We need someone fast, annoying, and smart to distract the asuras."

"So, obviously, it has to be me," Pooja said, expecting the denials which soon followed. "Think about it, ma'am.

I am, in your words, *the* most annoying person you have ever met. I am pretty smart and extremely quick. I am also small so I can escape quickly."

"No way in hell are you going to be the bait, this is final," Avi banged his fist on his lap.

"I agree with Avi on this," Arjun glared.

"Aw, look at you two getting along so well. Don't worry about me," she reached over and ruffled their hair.

"What if you are in trouble? What will we do then?" Ahan demanded.

"You come with me. If I go alone, the asuras might suspect that it's a distraction. If you are with me, they may think that only both of us came to get the book."

Ahan looked at Mahi. "It's not such a bad idea, actually. I was going to go alone, but she's right. Between the two of us, I think we can piss them off pretty fast. We will go around 200 meters and meet you near the turning."

"Alright, but be safe," Mahi cast a worried look at her husband.

"The people who should be the most concerned about safety are Arjun and Avi, considering you will be driving them," Pooja said, receiving a slap on the arm from her. "Hey, I was practicing being annoying, looks like I don't have to."

"You stick to the plan, don't make any detours. Take the book and come straight back to the van and meet us there. I love you," Ahan said, grabbing his bag. Pooja got her own out and tightened the ring around her finger, her weapon.

"I love you too," Mahi said just as Ahan pulled her in for a quick kiss. He looked up and gestured at the door. Pooja slid it open and stepped out into the cool evening air. She saw the sun sinking low.

"That's good for us," she said, pointing at the sun. "We will be harder to spot."

"You wish," Ahan gave her a dark smile. "Asuras can see perfectly in the dark. This will be a downside for us. They are stronger in the dark with night magic and stuff."

"Wait, don't I have night magic?" Pooja lifted a finger to prove her point.

"Can you control it?" Ahan smirked.

"Uh... no." Pooja's shoulders drooped as she pouted.

"Exactly." He hesitated before adding, "This is pretty dangerous. You can sit this one out."

"To feel helpless again? No way, I want to help. Partly to make this mission successful and partly to relieve me of my guilt about Thalia." Pooja mentally slapped herself for saying the last part out.

"Your friend's death wasn't your fault, Pooja," Ahan gently laid a hand on her shoulder.

"I know that, tell my feelings to stop feeling. They are stubborn; they won't listen to me."

Pooja jumped as the horn of the van sounded. Mahi yelled, "Get going or are you having second thoughts?"

"Come on," Ahan took one last look at his wife before dragging Pooja into the gathering.

Pooja held her breath as she peeked around the bushes they were hiding behind. She could hear the gruff chatter and laughter fill the air as men, who looked around 8-9 feet tall, clad in black traditional *dhotis*, roamed around the perimeter. They held sharp wooden spears almost 7 feet in length, which they occasionally swished around. Pooja spotted Mahi and the twins taking positions. Mahi looked at them and nodded.

Pooja and Ahan strode confidently into the gathering.

"Well, well, well, look who we have here. The husband of the Soul Tracker and the Princess, you will make a tasty dinner," an asura came forward. He was clearly the leader of the group, towering over them with an ugly crown made of leaves perched on his head, oily black hair falling down in chunks. His face was mostly covered with his mustache and beard, but his deep black eyes glinted with malice.

"I think we came to the wrong place, cousin," Pooja let out an incredulous laugh. "I heard asuras ate humans as soon as they saw them. What happened to these, are they the weak ones?"

"Perhaps they are scared that two humans can defeat them and send them back crying to their mommies," Ahan laughed. Pooja joined in, letting out a mean snicker. The scowl on the leader's face grew.

"We are not scared," he bellowed, spit flying in all directions. "Get them," he ordered two of his soldiers.

Pooja cursed under her breath. She hoped that their insults would rile up all the asuras, but they seemed to be more patient than she thought. Two asuras charged at Ahan and Pooja. Pooja immediately summoned her sword. She sidestepped as the asura swung his spear at her. The shaft buried itself into the ground. Pooja ran ahead and stabbed him straight in the heart. With a horrible wail, he melted into a puddle of flesh and blood that was slowly absorbed into the ground. Pooja turned to see Ahan, who was standing over his very own pile of flesh and blood, sword drawn.

"The asuras are losing their touch, maybe their wartime is over. Go back home and send your wives instead; they will do a better job. You stay home to please them after their victory," Ahan said, a challenging look in his eyes.

The asuras bellowed in anger, their egos were bruised too deeply. If they didn't charge, they would look weak and be laughed at. By whom? Well, ego doesn't let people, or asuras, think that far ahead.

"Charge!" the leader yelled, waving his spear around. Pooja flicked her sword, which turned back into a ring, turned, and fled. She ran through the grass, jumping over rocks and dodging holes in the ground. Pooja spotted the van, doors flung open with her companions thankfully in it. She ran straight toward it, hoping that Ahan was doing the same. She flung herself into the van and shut the door just as Ahan dove into the front seat.

"Go, go, go!" he urged as Mahi slammed her foot on the accelerator. The asuras gathered behind them, increasing their speed.

"Can't this thing go any faster?" Pooja asked desperately.

"This isn't built for a chase," Mahi groaned, "I'm going as fast as I can!"

"Well, it's not fast enough."

"Maybe we should eliminate the chase," Arjun's voice filled with steely determination. He punched a button on the roof of the van, which fell open completely. Arjun stood up, turned back, knocked an arrow in his bow, which he had conjured. He took aim, pulled the string, muscles flexing with the action, and let go of it. The arrow rushed through the air and slammed into the closest asura's heart. It took Arjun one minute to destroy the rest of the asuras, each arrow marking the target and bringing them down. This was the first time Pooja saw him in action, and it was breathtaking. The way his eyes flicked from target to target, his body adjusting itself so he could hit perfectly, and the way he bit his lower lip slightly in concentration sent an electric charge rushing down her spine.

"Wow, that was insane," she marveled, wide-eyed.

"Thanks," Arjun calmly sat back down, closing the sunroof, not even breathing hard. "So was your performance, by the way. You might have broken the world record for a two-hundred-meter race."

"Too bad nobody recorded it," Pooja shrugged.

"It would have been hard to explain the asuras," his dimples were back.

"Eh, who cares about fame anyway. Did you guys get the book?" Pooja turned to their companions.

"Yeah, the plan went smoothly on our side," Mahi said, with a little shake in her voice. It was obvious she was freaking out about what happened, even though she tried not to show it.

"Where is it?"

"With me," Avi leaned forward and showed the book to Pooja and Ahan, who turned his neck to look at it. The book was surprisingly normal; it was leather-bound, the size and shape of a photo album.

"Are you sure this is the one?" Ahan asked.

"Yeah, when you open this book, it shows you your family history. That's its specialty; it shows the family tree of the person opening the book," Avi informed.

"Well, that sucks. How are we supposed to know Prajwal's family tree?" Pooja's shoulders slumped in disappointment. She felt like she would lose it if their hard work went to waste.

"We have Prajwal's fingerprints in our system; we can use that to look at them. For now, take some rest. Tomorrow will be a big day," Mahi said.

Ahan took her free hand and kissed it lightly. "Good night," he said, placing her hand on his heart.

Pooja could almost feel Mahi's smile as she wished him good night back. Pooja felt her heart ache at their cuteness. They both were perfect for each other; they knew what the other person wanted without even needing to communicate. She had never seen a relationship so beautiful, so pure. She was scared of falling in love, scared that the man she would love would become a man like her father. A man she was scared of, a man she hated. More than that, she feared she would become like her mother, loving a man who doesn't deserve it, hoping that he would change even though it was clear he could never. The fates had given her a cruel childhood that made her value every small thing in life. She used to live in darkness, which made her appreciate the light.

"Ahan, let go of her hand. If we die in a van crash, I swear to the gods, I'll personally find you and kill you again," Pooja feigned panic because she didn't want to let her true feelings show.

"Hey, Pooja," Avi stopped the brawl before it began. "I just wanted to say I'm sorry. I was being a jerk; I was mad at my dad and was taking it out on you and Arjun. I never should have said the things I did; I hope you will forgive me."

"The near-death experience taught me that you shouldn't take silly things to heart. What is most important is to spend time with people you care about. Of course, I forgive you, Avi."

Pooja rested her head back on the seat, trying to clear her head and get some much-needed sleep. The van suddenly stopped, and Pooja's eyes snapped open with a jolt.

"This van has no suspension," she muttered to no one in particular, looking out of Avi's window and seeing a woman. She looked like she was in her late twenties, dressed in plain leggings and a kurta, her hair was cut short at her shoulder. She stood with her hands on her hips, blocking the path of the van.

"Sharanya," Ahan breathed.

"Prajwal's wife," Mahi confirmed.

"Excuse me? Prajwal's *wife*? Man, dude lucked out," Avi smirked as Pooja reached over and smacked his arm.

Sharanya made her way toward the van, as the light from one of the streetlights fell on her face. Pooja could see the shape she was in. Her lower lip was cut, bleeding slowly, as if the wound was a few days old. She looked like she hadn't slept in days, with bags under her eyes. Her right eye was bruised, and the front part of her hair looked like it had been tugged out. Her light brown skin looked golden in the warm light. Her eyes were desperate and wild. Her once beautiful blue kurta was tattered. Mahi rolled down her window.

"What happened to you?" she asked, her voice soft.

Sharanya bent forward so that she was face to face with Mahi. "This? I was caught trying to escape by my dear husband's guards. I have been waiting for you for a long time. I hope the asuras didn't give you a hard time,"

"No, they didn't," Ahan said. "They were useless, weak. Those asuras were not trained for battle or bloodshed."

"Of course not," Sharanya scoffed. "I was in charge of appointing the asuras to protect that book. I knew you would come for it; I needed you alive. I picked some of the young teenage rebels who wanted to fight instead of being slaves like their parents. I gave them the opportunity. Too bad you guys are way too experienced, right?"

"Why do you need us alive, Sharanya? And don't say it is because we were friends. You betrayed us all; you are not our friend anymore. I don't think you ever were," Mahi's voice cracked.

"I have my selfish reasons, but I need you safe. Do you mind if I come with you guys? I am unarmed; you guys can check me. I really need to rest, especially in my condition," her hand traveled to her belly, which was swollen, indicating her pregnancy.

"Of course," Mahi quickly replied.

After thoroughly checking Sharanya and confirming that she was neither bugged nor armed, Mahi made her squeeze in next to Pooja.

"While we are going to the Base, since we have nothing better to do, why don't you tell us why you need our help?" Ahan suggested.

"It's about helping Prajwal," Sharanya began.

"Save it, we are not helping that traitor," Ahan fumed.

"Oh gods, stop calling him that. It wasn't even his fault," she turned to Pooja, "Back me up here."

"What? Why would I back you up?" Pooja incredulously asked.

"Don't act all innocent; you were young then, but you would definitely remember even now. In that room, he summoned the spirit..."

Sharanya's voice muffled as Pooja was sucked into the Bermuda Triangle of her memories.

....

"Okay," Prajwal whispered, "Almost done."

Pooja was in an excited Prajwal's arms. His eyes were shining with happiness as he cooed at her.

"We are going to do this, Pooja. I will help you save the world just like my ancestor helped yours. Isn't that great?" he cooed.

Pooja babbled excitedly and squealed as Prajwal bounced her, grinning.

"We just need some of our blood," he set Pooja down. Crouching low, he produced a dagger. Pooja immediately reached out for it, wanting to put it in her mouth.

"Now, now, you can't eat this. You will get hurt; we don't want that now, do we?" Prajwal sliced his palm and watched the blood slowly trickle down his hand.

Pooja touched his wound with her baby hands. "Boo-boo," she looked up for signs of pain on Prajwal's face.

"Yes, but it's a small boo-boo. Now, we need some of yours. Show me your hand," he gently took Pooja's hand and made a small cut. Pooja looked at her skin slicing open in awe, then the pain hit her and she began crying.

"Shh, you can handle a little pain," Prajwal picked her up and placed his hand on a circular door with the face of an extremely hairy man and pushed it open. They entered a circular, dimly lit chamber. Pooja stopped crying as she felt a powerful presence that sent shivers down her spine. She pressed herself closer to Prajwal, who was practically jumping in joy. He walked to the centre of the chamber and placed his palm in the middle of an extremely complicated design made up of chalk powder. He let some blood collect in the middle and repeated the process with Pooja's hand. He began chanting loudly in Sanskrit, and the blood began to glow brighter; the cold presence seemed to grow stronger. The wall began to crack in front of them.

Prajwal smiled, "I summon Prajwal Borkar!" There was silence; the cracks on the wall began to spread. With a loud bang that startled Pooja, blue light filled the room.

"Prajwal, you have truly proved yourself to be worthy of my name," a voice boomed.

"Thank you, sire. I wanted to summon you so that you could help me protect the world, be the right hand man to the Prince and Princess who were, fortunately for me, born in my time," Prajwal stared at the light with wonder.

"You fool," the voice chuckled, "The Prince and Princess are nothing but a lie. The gods don't deserve to rule the world; it's time they step down and let the asuras rule."

"What?" Prajwal's smile dimmed, and he took a small step back.

"Boy, you have so much to learn. You and I together, we can destroy the gods and help the rightful rulers of the world ascend the throne."

"You are crazy," Prajwal snuggled Pooja closer and backed away. "Go away!"

The blue light swirled together, forming a huge body of power: tall and foreboding, evil.

"Go away, I banish you! Go back to hell, where you truly belong!" Prajwal roared, shielding Pooja with his body.

The deep laughter let out by the spirit of Prajwal's ancestor echoed through the room, making it sound more evil, more powerful. "There is no going back now," the blue light rushed toward Prajwal.

"No!" he whimpered, placing Pooja safely on the ground and putting as much distance between her as he could, trying to escape the light. Unfortunately, he was too slow. The light crashed into him, flinging him to the other side of the wall. The room rumbled as the cracks spread around the chamber, ready to collapse.

Prajwal stood up groggily, staring at his body. He stood up tentatively and sank back down, holding his head, screaming in pain. Terrified, Pooja began to crawl toward him, crying for her mother.

"Stay back," Prajwal hissed. He groaned as his body shuddered violently. He looked like he was losing control over his actions. Taking some calming breaths, he rested his back on the wall, pushed his head up, and let out a slow breath. Opening his eyes, filled to the brim with tears, he stood up slowly and began pacing the room worriedly, head bent low.

Prajwal looked up. He looked terrified, messing up his brown curls, mumbling incoherently, "I don't know what to do. I feel like it is embracing me forcefully, taking control of my whole being. I don't want to hurt anyone. Maybe I should have never gone through that damned book. I should've just listened. I want Mahi and Ahan to be safe. They were nothing but kind to me." His eyes bore into Pooja's, haunted yet determined.

"Promise me you will protect them no matter what. I know you can."

"Pooja!" Arjun's voice rang in her ears. Pooja frowned. What was Arjun doing here?

She opened her eyes and found herself staring into Arjun's concerned blue ones. She pushed herself up to see that the van had stopped. Mahi, Ahan, Sharanya, and Avi were all standing outside the door, looking at her worriedly. Arjun was standing closest to her.

"What happened?" Pooja asked, her brain aching from reliving the memory. She felt tears in her eyes, which she quickly wiped.

"I was talking to you about the room, and you collapsed and started shaking. We were so scared we thought you were going to have a seizure or something worse," Sharanya's voice shook. Pooja could tell that whatever happened terrified her companions.

"I had a, um, flashback of my memory," she rubbed her aching temple.

"Oh man, does it look like this?" Ahan shuddered.

"Yeah, Ahan filled me in on the memory-losing part and all the crazy stuff," Sharanya licked her lips nervously. "What did you see?"

"Prajwal wasn't a bad person; he is in this phase of killing the devas due to an experiment that failed horribly," Pooja started. She explained everything she had relived in detail, all about the crazy ritual that Prajwal did, the fear in his eyes when he realized his mistake, the fact that he was possessed by his psycho namesake.

"Oh gods, Prajwal must have been so scared," Mahi sighed.

"He was possessed by his crazy ancestor. I believe he is making Prajwal do all this nonsense, ending what he started in his lifetime," Ahan's eyes widened in horror.

"He is capable enough to do so. Prajwal the First was killed by a man who realized his true intentions. The man we think was the monster who was trying to end Pooja's ancestor, the Last Hope, we call him, was the one actually trying to save him. I had no idea who Prajwal summoned, now I do," Sharanya pursed her lips tightly.

"What do you need Mahi ma'am for?" Pooja asked.

"I was hoping that she could exorcise the spirit, but she can't."

"What? Why not?"

"Well, since we know that it was you and Prajwal who brought the spirit back to Earth, it can only be the two of you who can send him back," Mahi explained.

"We have to get the possessed Prajwal to work with me?" Pooja exclaimed in disbelief, "Like that's gonna happen."

"It has to, that's how you can save the world, and my husband," Sharanya looked at Pooja with pleading eyes. Pooja felt pity toward Prajwal's situation; all he wanted to do was help, but instead, he became the problem. She sighed deeply; she knew she had to put her hatred for Prajwal aside and focus on the world, but she was only human. She hoped that she wouldn't lose control of her emotions when she faced Prajwal, especially because he's the reason her friend was no more.

"I will, but you need to answer me honestly. The day Prajwal ambushed us at school, what did he want?" Pooja asked. This was the one question she needed an answer to. She had to know what was so important that her friend had to die.

"The spirit wanted Prajwal to marry Mahi, as you know. Prajwal didn't want to marry her because he loves me. It was an ongoing battle between the two until finally, the spirit won. Prajwal tracked down Mahi at the school and ambushed her. You were never supposed to be there, but recruiting the Princess, or holding her hostage would be a huge advantage to the spirit's sick cause. Mahi was mandatorily supposed to bend her knee to the spirit; you would be the icing on the cake."

Pooja nodded. She never broke her promise before, and she wasn't planning on doing it anytime soon. She would partner with Prajwal, the man whose gruesome death she fantasized about, in order to make sure the asuras wouldn't win.

Avi reached out and squeezed her arm, "Remember who the enemy is, not Prajwal, but the asuras. If the asuras didn't want to rule the world, Prajwal Borkar the First would never have tried to kill our ancestor, possess your sister-in-law's ex, or be responsible for your friend's death."

"Nobody but me is responsible for Thal's death," Pooja voiced the thought that had been eating her alive. The guilt slammed into her, and her lip trembled as she tried to get a grip on herself.

"No, don't you ever think that," Ahan pulled Pooja into a side hug. "You were helping us. You couldn't have known that the minion of Prajwal would shoot an innocent, unarmed child. Stop blaming yourself for things that are not even remotely your fault."

"Sorry," Pooja sniffed, "I'm making this whole thing about myself, when it shouldn't even matter. These small things are nothing compared to the whole world ending. I'm being selfish, I shouldn't be having an emotional breakdown right now."

"I assume it's safe to say that your therapy is going quite well, now that you are able to comfortably speak about your emotions," Mahi smiled at her with pride.

This was true. Dr Camara had been most helpful in breaking the emotional walls Pooja built for herself so she wouldn't go mad because of her abusive father. Thrice a week, she was forced to talk about her emotions and feelings. Suddenly not going to therapy made her unstable and talk about her feelings at the wrong time, like now. She imagined Dr Camara's reaction if she saw her now, spilling her emotions to people she met only recently. She would call it progress; the old Pooja would call it weakness.

Pooja didn't trust herself to speak, afraid she might cry, so she smiled back at her teacher in agreement. Ahan rubbed her arm comfortingly before snatching the keys from Mahi.

"The way you are driving, stopping every five minutes, we will reach the base by next year. I'll drive, it will be smooth," he smiled cockily, to which Mahi rolled her eyes.

Everyone got back into the van and crashed immediately, exhausted. Pooja was wide awake, staring out of the window into the darkness, watching the summer raindrops falling like tears from the sky. She kept thinking about how she, a kid with no idea how her powers were supposed to work, would save the world from an attack from one of the most powerful creatures to exist.

WHO THOUGHT MAKEUP
WAS A GOOD IDEA?

"No way," Indra was fuming, pacing in his study.

As soon as the party reached the base, they were immediately called to return the book. Indra nearly had a heart attack and ordered his guards to kill her when Sharanya entered the chamber of the king. Arjun and Avi had to physically force him into the chair so he could be caught up to date. As expected, Indra took a while to trust Sharanya's story, but eventually, he had to admit there was an undeniable logic to it.

Pooja sighed, "Think about it, Your Highness. I didn't even grow up here; people will have a hard time trusting me because of this. You wanted a great thing to happen that would make people trust me without a second thought. Prajwal is considered to be a monster; imagine if I take him down and get him back to the base where he fights alongside us during the Final War. What could be more heroic than that?"

"You have a point," Indra admitted, "But you don't have the proper training to complete an exorcism. That is extremely difficult to do; in fact, it has only been done once before. The man who did it gave up 20 years of his life to achieve this extraordinary thing."

"Well, the dude who did it wasn't the Princess," Pooja countered. She knew this argument was pathetic, but she was willing to do anything to convince him.

"Fine, but I have conditions."

"Anything."

"Firstly, since you need training, I will contact the guy who performed the exorcism to come and train you. He is highly capable and has proved himself to be loyal to the throne multiple times. However, to be his student, you must prove your worth, so prepare yourself. He values commitment, discipline, and loyalty the most, so work on those skills.

"Secondly, we will announce to the public that you are the Princess and you will be going to end the looming threat named Prajwal.

"Thirdly, you will be transferred from your current sleeping quarters to wherever your new trainer wants you to be.

"Fourthly, since your new trainer specializes in one-on-one, for a certain period of time, he will decide whom you meet and when you meet them. He will control everything you do from when you wake up until you sleep. He might even control your dreams.

"Lastly, the training you will receive will be vigorous and will demand everything from you. What we want here is for you to learn something that you would learn in six years usually in only around six months. You will fully grasp the powers of Yama during this time. It's no joke, since you've had exactly zero training. He will prepare you both physically and mentally for facing Prajwal. Even after all this, there are high chances you might fail, and by fail, I mean die. Are you ready for it?"

"Yeah, I guess," Pooja hesitated. "This is a lot, but I'm confident that I might be able to do it."

"Alright, then," Indra stood up. "You can't go back to the dorms, so I will have someone get your stuff for you. You will move back to the guest room immediately. Arjun, Avi, you will answer no questions about Pooja; say it's classified. The same goes for you, Mr and Mrs Singh. Tomorrow there will be a ceremony where Pooja will be officially declared Princess; attendance is mandatory. Sharanya, you will have to stay in the guest quarters and not have contact with anyone for your own safety. That's all; everyone can leave."

As Pooja, Avi, and Arjun began to head downstairs together, Mahi called out, "Pooja, a word?"

"Sure," she turned to the twins. "You guys go ahead. I'll catch you later, hopefully."

Mahi approached her, "It's about your new trainer. This guy guided me in my pursuit of powers back when I was studying here. I know a couple of things you can do to get in his good books if you want to know."

"Has there ever been an instance where you have not helped me?" Pooja mused. "Yes, I want to know and thank you for this."

"If you really are the Princess, we all have to thank you for saving the world. I'm going to be happy I aided you in some way."

"Yeah, about the trainer?" Pooja changed the topic, wary of the respect she was getting for a title she hadn't earned.

"Yeah, so, his name is Ramesh Patel. He looks scary, but he is actually kind-hearted. As long as you aren't intimidated by him, you can see how much of a good man he is. He will put in 100% effort to help you and won't take credit until you give it to him. He is specially trained in every form of weaponry, which, I assume, will be part of your training. Practice your basics, be thorough with them. He will scare you to death, but you must show willpower. It's okay if you can't do something; at least try it. He admires risk-takers and a never-going-to-give-up attitude."

"Meaning he's going to love me," Pooja smiled.

"Sure, kid," Mahi smirked. "I don't know when we will meet again, so good luck."

"Wait, I have a doubt."

"Yeah?"

"Since I have to train with this Ramesh guy, does that mean I don't have to attempt my half-yearly exams?"

"Yeah, you'll be excused."

"Mahi didn't write her final exams in our last year because she was in training with Ramesh," Ahan informed. "While we were working our asses off, she was literally chilling with him. It still makes me mad."

"He's jealous," Mahi beat his arm lightly.

Pooja smiled. She would miss them and bid them adieu as they made their way to the teacher's quarters. Slowly, she trudged to the guest quarters, gave her name at the reception, and went to her room. She showered and crashed immediately.

The next morning, she was woken up by a group of people huddled outside her room.

"Hello," a woman said. Her jet-black hair was curled to perfection and fell to her waist with brown highlights. Her face was flawless and sparkling, her smile would make anyone smile back at her... except Pooja.

"What?" she asked.

"Ms Pooja Bahl?" she asked.

"Yeah, who are you?"

"We are a few Kamadevs, we are here to prepare you for the Princess announcement party."

The group brushed past her and began setting up their things in her room. Grumbling, Pooja went to freshen up. By the time she was done trying to look presentable, her room looked like a beauty salon; there were stations for hairdressing, manicures, pedicures, clothes, and other stuff she didn't even recognize.

She was given some water before they began to assault her. She was forced into a robe which, as they informed, would make it comfortable for her to be dressed. Every inch of her was covered with beauty products and whatnot. By the time they were done, Pooja was already exhausted to the core.

"Is that it?" she asked, her voice hopeful.

"Yep, that's all," another woman answered. Pooja couldn't believe her luck and almost smiled until another woman dashed her hopes.

"We just have to do your hair and pick your outfit."

Pooja's hair was thoroughly washed, gels were applied to it, washed again, more gels applied to it. It was brushed out, dried, and styled until her hair fell in beautiful waves down to her lower back.

After going through several outfits, Pooja found one that literally took her breath away. There was a beautiful silk sari; it was blood red with black borders. Pooja looked strong, regal, and powerful in it, and she could see herself as a future ruler. Pooja wore a black and silver choker, a silver bracelet, and her grandfather's ring, making her look simple yet regal. As she looked at herself in the mirror, Pooja didn't see a 13-year-old child. Instead, she saw a warrior princess, someone who can easily destroy or save the world.

"Wow, this is amazing," Pooja sighed wistfully, twirling around.

"Of course it is, we are the best at our job," a man dressed in sparkling clothes replied.

Pooja turned around to see the Kamadevs packing their stuff away.

"Thank you all for taking the time to get me ready for this," she smiled, to which they exchanged surprised glances. "What happened? Did I say something wrong?"

"No, Princess," a woman with perfect curls clarified, "We just don't get appreciated very often."

"Well, you should, I mean," Pooja gestured at herself, "You've transformed me from a wild beast into a beautiful princess."

Exchanging bemused glances, they left. Pooja sank into her bed, 'Great, you've weirded out these people as well. Next time, just keep your mouth shut,' she thought. She heard someone knock on her door. She pulled herself up to her feet and pulled the door open. Outside stood Arjun. He was wearing a beautiful cream dhoti, which was simple yet made him look royal. He wore a silver chain and a bangle. His beautiful deep blue eyes were lined with kohl, which made them almost as striking as the smile he was wearing. The same smile that got Pooja's throat drying up and the butterflies in her stomach throwing a party. He wasn't wearing an *angavastram*, displaying his toned muscles and abs. He was *thirteen* and he had *abs*. Four of them. He stood tall, almost 2 meters, his waves styled in a fashionable mess. He smelled like mud after rain, a smell Pooja oddly loved. She opened her mouth to say something but closed it again because she couldn't think of one thing that would sound appropriate.

"You look..." Arjun's voice was deep and husky. He cleared his throat. "You look gorgeous."

Pooja blinked, feeling like a complete idiot. "You look pretty. I mean, good. You smell nice."

"I smell nice?" Arjun repeated slowly.

"Yeah? New cologne?" Pooja turned beet red in embarrassment. She looked down, unable to maintain eye contact.

Arjun chuckled, "Yeah, it is. I usually don't smell like this."

"Yup, you smell like the ocean breeze usually," Pooja realized that she was sounding like a creep; to avoid further embarrassment, she changed the topic. "So, why are you here and where is Avi?"

"I'm here to escort you to the party, it's kind of a formality. I'm your guide to royal life, you could say. You hang on to my arm, I introduce you to ministers at my dad's court, you make small talk, we leave. We get to spend the whole afternoon and evening like so. Avi has other responsibilities, like welcoming the guests and being the one to officially initiate your pre-coronation."

"Pre-coronation?"

"You will basically be crowned as the princess officially. Your main coronation will be as a queen with your king, after marriage."

"Marriage? I have to marry you?"

Arjun gave her a sly smile, "It won't be *that* bad." He laughed at the horrified look on Pooja's face, "We are not sure about anything, but mostly it will come up to that, dad will decide. You will have to make the choice about who you want as a life partner, and the person who helps you save the world... me or Avi. Just out of curiosity, who would you pick?"

"I'd marry myself," Pooja decided. That wasn't necessarily true.

Arjun chuckled softly.

THE PRE-CORONATION (THAT EXISTS?)

The party took place in the sorting room because of two reasons. The first being that it was only appropriate for the gods to witness the officiating of one of the two saviors of the world. The second being it was the only room big enough where the whole population of the base could fit in.

Even though everybody was supposed to attend the party mandatorily, after the pre-coronation Pooja was supposed to tour the entire base to 'bless' it with her presence. The only three exciting things about this, according to Pooja, were that she could finally see how life was outside the castle, she would be allowed to ride her winged horse which she had befriended when she was younger, and Arjun was going to be there. The last one was *only* because Arjun kept her entertained.

As they neared the entrance, Arjun stopped her, and they stood, staring at the closed double oak doors.

"What's the wait? Let's go inside," Pooja leaned forward to push open the doors.

"Don't be dumb," Arjun pleaded, "There is an entrance music for you."

"Oh gods, that's too much."

"There are people inside who have been waiting for your arrival since they were babies. They have a lot of expectations from you, and you have to act like you've got your shit together, especially now. People might do crazy things like touching your feet; don't look disturbed by that. Show them you can handle this like a pro," he squeezed her hand. "I believe in you."

Pooja wished Arjun would stop saying nice things like that because the butterflies in her stomach always got overexcited when he did. Hell, they got overexcited as soon as they saw him. Pooja pushed those thoughts from her head just in time; the trumpets started blaring from inside the hall, and Pooja straightened her back and took a deep breath as the doors swung open.

It was like a scene from the movies, as Pooja and Arjun glided across the room on a red carpet. There were cheers, cries, and prayers thrown at them from the crowd. Pooja's head began to spin as the crowd kept closing in, desperate to get their voices heard. She tightened her grip around Arjun's hand and managed to maintain a calm look as she practically ran across to Avi, Indra, and Ayeesha who were waiting for them on the dais.

Arjun led her to the centre and stood next to his brother, who was dressed in a similar dhoti with an *angavastram* lazily draped on his right shoulder. He wore pearl earrings, which traditionally matched his attire. Indra was dressed in a pure white dhoti with intricate designs and sparkle. He wore manly golden chains and earrings with a crown atop his head. While his sons were dressed simply, he was dressed royally. His wife was no exception, dressed in gold and red; she looked striking, like a queen. The confidence she held herself with made Pooja feel like a cheap con artist, pretending she could rule this place. However, when she met Pooja's eyes, her eyebrows raised in approval and gave her an encouraging smile, which Indra mirrored. She realized that she was expected to say something. Great.

She looked at the crowd and cleared her throat; her voice magically magnified. The chatter in the hall stopped immediately, and she felt the eyes of hundreds of people on her. She closed her eyes and took a deep breath. She had anchored in her school cultural programs before; she could close her eyes and imagine she was there.

"Hello everyone, I would like to personally thank each and every one of you for showing up to this event. Let me be honest with you, when I was first told I was supposed to lead you all to win a war, I wasn't sure I was capable of doing it. I wasn't sure if I deserved to lead a wonderful, courageous army like you all. Now, I am sure as hell that I am not."

There were shocked gasps from the crowd.

"Tell me, people, what have I done to deserve your trust?" she continued over the surprised chatter, which stopped immediately. "Nothing. I haven't proven my worth to you all, and I can't ask you to follow me into a battle which decides the fate of you and your loved ones. I see you before me, so strong, so full of love, so human, and I know that winning your trust will be winning half the battle for me. You guys should fight and die for a person you know with full confidence will fight and die for you. My fellow citizens, I am ready to fight and die for you. These are not mere words, in case any of you are thinking that. I am going to prove myself by defeating Prajwal Borkar."

There was a pin-drop silence, long enough to make Pooja rethink her choice of words. Maybe they thought she was joking. Maybe they expected something more from her. Maybe she should've said hi and shut up. Then, the crowd started clapping, cheering for her. They were chanting her name in reverence, respect, and love. Pooja had won the heart of every single citizen of the Base.

"Thank you," she stepped back, and Avi took her position. He tried to speak, but the crowd drowned out his voice; they were too loud.

"You did such a good job, Pooja. I'm proud of you," Indra smiled down at her. She smiled back. As she looked at the crowd, she couldn't stop smiling.

Arjun slipped his hand into hers. "I knew you had it in you. Where's the party after your immense success?"

"This *is* the party," she laughed.

Finally, once the crowd was silenced, Avi began to speak, "As the Princess has declared, she will be going to defeat Prajwal Borkar once and for all." Another cheer went up from the crowd. "Today, in front of the gods, we will be officially recognizing our Princess. Let the ceremony begin with the acting king's blessing."

Indra took his son's place. "As the Princess has returned, we can only assume the Final War will happen soon. We must be grateful and honored that each and every one of us can have the honor of fighting for the devas against the asuras. We all can defeat whatever threat they pose because we fight for dharma, we fight with unity, we fight with love. *Satya, dharma Vijaya prapthirasthu!*"

"*Satya, dharma Vijaya prapthirasthu!*" the crowd roared. May truth and dharma be victorious.

The pre-coronation ceremony was quite long. Pooja had to vow to try her best to follow the path of dharma and put the citizens' needs before her own. She had to swear that she would never go behind the backs of the citizens and dedicate her life to ensuring the victory of dharma with the gods as her witnesses. Then, she was sprinkled with water from the Ganges River and had to witness a yagna, a sacrificial ritual where ghee is poured into the fire for the gods. There were priests gathered around, chanting hymns that calmed her nerves.

Pooja could finally relax and observe her surroundings, unlike when she first came here. The wall was decorated with marigold flowers that emitted a sweet smell around the room. There were mango leaves placed around the sacrificial fire, and of course, there were more designs made with chalk powder. She sat down on the dais on a mat along with the royal family. The citizens either sat on the floor, on chairs, or helped themselves to the buffet. The smells wafting from the food centre made Pooja's mouth water and stomach rumble. She hadn't eaten food as per the traditions required since morning, and she was facing the consequences. Mustering all her willpower, she looked away from the food and found Avi staring at her with a smile.

"What?" she whispered so as not to disturb the holy aura of the room.

"You do realize that the love of your life will be the Prince, right?" he whispered back.

"Yeah, Arjun told me that. What about it?"

"I don't think biryani will be such a great leader, you know."

"Shut up," Pooja smacked Avi.

"Children, now is really not the time," Indra spoke in a low but stern voice.

"Sorry," Avi and Pooja chorused.

After the festivities were complete, Avi walked up to thank the guests for coming on behalf of the royal family. Pooja went around exchanging pleasantries with the royal ministers and their families. She shook hands until it felt like her arms would fall off. Throughout all this, Arjun once again proved himself to be the Golden Boy by striking up conversations and actually looking interested in what people had to say. After they had completed the greetings, they were both ushered outside the palace through a side door Pooja didn't even know existed. As they walked to the stables, a servant rushed up to them with two bags and handed one to each.

"What's in this?" she asked him. The servant teared up, touched her feet in reverence, and left quickly without answering her question. Pooja stared at him as he quickly disappeared out of sight.

"Clothes," Arjun said, "As much as I love looking at you in that, you can't ride with it on. You need something more appropriate."

Pooja nodded, her heart thumping. "You should probably change too; we don't want girls walking into each other, drooling over you."

"Thank you," Arjun grinned, "I'll change, don't be jealous of other girls." He shot her a wink and left. Pooja blushed and looked around for a place to change. She found a women's restroom and went inside.

The bag had a lilac silk jumpsuit, a hair tie of the same color, and wet wipes. Pooja cleaned the makeup and sweat from her face and put on the jumpsuit. She tied her hair into a high pony and looked at herself in the mirror. She didn't look like a princess anymore; she looked like a common rich girl. She understood what her wardrobe designers were trying to do. They were conveying that Pooja might be the princess, but at heart she is just like the citizens, a normal Blessed, making them trust her like she was one of their own.

Pooja stepped out and waited for a while until Arjun arrived in a lilac shirt and black jeans.

He looked at Pooja with a smile, "You will love this ride."

He didn't lie. Once the winged horse recognized Pooja's scent, it went crazy, licking her, whining, and jumping around. Pooja fed it an apple given by the stable boy, and it ate it up quickly.

"This stallion's name is Shadow," Arjun informed her while petting the horse. His coat was dark as night, making him the perfect companion for a stealth mission in the dark.

Pooja mounted the steed and walked it around a little to get control of the animal. Arjun was atop a gray one with blue eyes. "Say hi to Thunder," he urged his horse to gallop around Pooja.

"Let's race to the palace gates?" Arjun asked.

"No way, I don't know where they are," Pooja laughed at Arjun's excitement.

"No worries, follow me. I'm afraid you might find it hard to keep up," he spurred his horse and galloped at a high speed. Pooja knew instantly that horse riding was Arjun's favorite hobby. Pooja had taken horse riding classes when she was young, so she had no trouble keeping up with Arjun. By the time they made it out of the palace, horses and riders both were exhilarated.

"That was awesome," Arjun grinned almost crazily. "Isn't this wonderful?"

"It is," Pooja sighed, "we should do it more often, but now I really think we should start with the tour."

"Yeah, the tour," Arjun fell in pace with Pooja's horse as they roamed around the base. It was arranged in a symmetrical way where each god had a specific area to themselves. Each area had a temple worshipping the god, and houses themed in the god's colors. All houses were exactly the same, simple yet luxurious, with bronze plates numbering them. Almost in the centre of the base were things for amusement such as malls, theatres, and parks. These were used by everyone, but it was empty that particular day. It seemed like people were still attending the function.

"So, what do you think of our humble abode?" Arjun asked as they neared the end of the base. The end was a beach, the calm waves crashing onto the shore just like the one seen from the palace.

"This place is too formal, everything about life in the Base is formal," Pooja commented.

Arjun dismounted his horse and began walking it toward a tree. Pooja followed suit.

"You must understand one thing, Pooja. No matter how much this place seems welcoming and comfortable, remember that this is basically a military camp. Even after graduating from the Base school, there are compulsory drills once every week. Every man and woman here is fit and trained to either fight or heal for the Final War," Arjun's shoulders slumped as he tied Thunder to the tree.

"That's not right. You are telling me that kids grow up in a military lifestyle? What about the parks and malls?" Pooja asked, surprised, as she tied Shadow to a neighbouring tree.

Arjun didn't answer but led Pooja to the beach. He sat down on the shore, stretched out, putting one hand behind his head. Pooja fell onto the sand next to him and closed her eyes, listening to Arjun's soft breathing and the calming sound of the ocean waves.

"There is not much we can do about it," Arjun finally murmured. "I have been envious of the lifestyle you had, the freedom you had before the Base. As for the entertainment things, everything is scheduled. They are accessible only on weekends, and even then, you have to inform the authorities beforehand what you plan to do. This place is basically a luxurious prison."

"No way," Pooja propped herself on one elbow, turning to Arjun. "I'm the Princess, this means that the Final War is going to happen soon. People have to live the last years of their lives, if they have years, that is, properly. They are basically pigs raised for slaughter."

Arjun smiled a sad smile and cupped Pooja's face. "You are absolutely right, we are pigs being raised for slaughter. We have no purpose in this life except fighting the Final War, and people have already accepted that. As the War is nearing, unity and discipline are the most important things for us right now. Changing your basic lifestyle will affect their performance, which might just tip the scales in the asuras' favour."

"You sound just like your father," Pooja fumed. She hated how resigned Arjun sounded.

Dropping his hand, he said in a hard voice, "Maybe I am just a clone of his."

"Let's not do this right now," Pooja lay back down. "Let's not fight, please. Let's just enjoy this while it lasts. We have to go back soon, anyway."

Arjun sighed but didn't say anything.

"I'm sorry," Pooja apologized.

"Don't give me hope, Pooja. Don't give me hope that my life can be better, because once I begin to agree with you, I can't be happy with what I have. That will ruin me, the life I've built here," his voice cracked.

"But it can, I can help you. All you have to do is cooperate, please," she pleaded.

"What are you going to do? Your new guru is coming tomorrow and is going to take you with him. I won't even see you. What will I do with hope when I can't do anything with it? It is hopeless."

Pooja knew he was right, but she didn't want Arjun to miss any more of his childhood. He had a pure heart and deserved a happy life. Deep down, she knew the lifestyle of the Base helped it survive in the past, but now? Now they have to live.

"When I come back with Prajwal, we will do something about it. We will rule as per our terms, we won't give too much freedom, but not restrict it either. This will help our citizens make the right decisions during do-or-die moments."

Arjun smiled slyly.

"What? You agree?" Pooja asked hopefully.

"Yeah. It looks like you have decided who will rule with you, huh?"

"Of course, we both make a good team and we can rule without marriage. Your father said as much."

"My father will say anything to convince people, but he won't lie. He didn't say you wouldn't marry one of us, he said Krishna didn't mention marriage. Let's not kid anyone, we know that you will have to marry whoever you choose to rule alongside you. Avi and I have been telling you this the whole time."

"Yeah, I thought you were joking," Pooja frowned, hurt at how easily she was manipulated into thinking that her life was on her terms. She wondered how Arjun and Avi dealt with this since childhood. She turned and hugged him, face pressed against his shoulder. Startled, Arjun held her shoulder hesitantly, but pushed himself up to hug her back.

"I am so sorry, I shouldn't have brought it up so abruptly," Pooja closed her eyes.

"It's alright," Arjun patted her head awkwardly and cleared his throat. "I don't mind talking about these kinds of things with you, to be honest. It feels like a huge weight is being lifted off my shoulders."

"I'm glad I could help," she said as she pulled away. "I have a doubt. Are there any more kids who joined the training at the Education Centre when they were kids apart from Avi and you?"

"Yeah, there are many kids like me."

"How come I haven't met anybody? I go to all classes with the same people, and all of them are newly recruited."

"You are smart," Arjun smiled softly, "I'll give you two minutes to think about that."

"Wait, we are divided based on our knowledge, not age. This means that all the people who joined as little kids will be studying with you."

"Yes, genius. The things you are learning right now, I learnt when I was six years old."

"Arjun, can you do something for me?" Pooja straightened up and looked into his eyes. He could say no; so many bad things could happen if she continued, but she knew that it was the right thing to do.

"Of course, anything."

"After I leave tomorrow, you need to go ask people in your learning group how they feel about the whole thing. Keep it casual; I need to know how the people are feeling or I won't be a good ruler. If many people don't like it and feel like they are being forced to do something, their performance in the war won't be good. If they are unsatisfied, we might lose the war, and I will not let that happen."

"Pooja, this will be difficult. My dad won't support this."

"I am the Princess who will come back after turning Prajwal good. What has your father done except for sitting on his throne and enforcing laws on his citizens? Who do you think the citizens will trust, me or your dad?"

"You," Arjun stood up. Pooja followed suit. "We have to go now." He didn't move. He stared wistfully at the ocean and then looked back at Pooja. She felt her heart flutter as he stepped close. He leaned forward, "You are the blessing this Base desperately requires."

RAMESH PATEL

Pooja lay in bed, it was almost midnight, her covers up to her chin. After the short break at the beach, Pooja and Arjun rode back, went into the hall, and feasted with the royal family. Pooja went to meet Mahi and Ahan; they spoke about Ramesh Patel for a while. Pooja went to meet her classmates at the end. They were all gathered in the fitness grounds, waiting for her arrival. As soon as she came, she was greeted by an enthusiastic Vinay.

"You are the Princess? Oh my God, I got slapped by our leader!"

"What are you talking about?" Pooja frowned. She would have remembered slapping him because she found him annoying and she really wished to do it.

"That day you were talking to Meher and backhanded me."

"That was an accident, doesn't count."

Before Vinay could give a reply, she was swarmed by her other classmates.

"You looked so pretty during the pre-coronation," Eshan squealed.

"You didn't even tell us you were the Princess," Aarav grumbled.

"Do you remember me?" Sooraj asked.

"I always liked you; we should be friends," Tarak, a guy who used to pick on Meher and Pooja, smiled.

Things like, "you are so brave," "your speech was inspiring," and "you are the best choice to lead us," were said by all of them. She could only remember a few of the kids' names, since they didn't bother with her before. It hurt Pooja how fast everyone wanted to get to know her now that she was in power, when she was the quiet kid in the back of the room before nobody even looked at her. Power can twist people's minds and change their loyalties, which scared Pooja. She pushed her way through the crowd, murmuring thank-yous as fake as the compliments, looking for Meher. She found her standing at the end, arms folded, glowering at the crowd. She saw Pooja approaching and her frown deepened.

"What?" she demanded as soon as Pooja was within earshot.

"I am so sorry, Meher."

"You should be. You are the Princess, and you didn't even bother telling me about that. What was I? A project to know how the citizens think about the Royals? You talk about how you hate lies and backstabbing people. What are you now? Was being my friend all an act?" she fumed.

"Of course it wasn't. Meher, you are one of my closest friends here, in fact, you were the only one who befriended me for me, not my title. I really should have told you, but I was also recruited recently. Not that it is any excuse, but I was scared of what might happen if I told you. Indra wanted it to be a secret. I didn't know what to do, so I did what he told me to do; it seemed easier then. I am so very sorry."

"You need to stop doing that."

"Stop doing what?"

"Being so nice," Meher tried but failed to bite back a smile, "you are making it difficult for me to be mad at you."

"Does that mean you forgive me?" Pooja grinned back.

"Not yet, you have six more months to make it up to me."

"Actually, no," Pooja told her about how she was leaving to train with Ramesh Patel.

"You need training? When you declared you would defeat Prajwal, I assumed you were already trained. That you lied to me about researching about the secret room and trained instead."

"No, that's a very smart thing to do so obviously the Royals didn't think of it."

"Don't say that, someone might overhear you," Meher looked around cautiously.

"What will they do? I hold the highest power here," Pooja flexed.

"Okay, Princess," Meher chuckled, "What will be the first thing you will do as a Princess?"

"Unlimited dessert privileges for all," Pooja answered quickly. Chuckling, both of them walked toward the castle, chatting with each other.

Pooja sat next to Meher for dinner even though Indra sent guards to beg her to sit with the Royals. She knew that she wouldn't regret even a second, she spent with Meher, and she was right. Before she went to the King's Chamber, as instructed, Meher broke down in tears.

"You must think I'm a baby right now," she chuckled through her tears, "But I am going to miss you. After the training, you are going to go straight to Prajwal's place and fight him alone. That scares me. I know you can defeat him, but please be careful. It will suck if you die. I really love you a lot, and you are my closest friend. Just remember this, if you feel like things are not going your way, at least know that you are not alone anymore. You have people who would die for you and love you the same way you love them." She reached forward and pulled Pooja into a hug. Not the usual side hugs, but a proper, meaningful one.

Pooja stiffened, but soon relaxed and hugged her back, "I needed to hear that. Thank you. I love you too." She smiled at Meher and left quickly, not wanting Meher to see the tears that were rolling down her cheeks.

Soon, she reached the King's Chamber and knocked thrice, surprised to see no guards present outside as they usually were.

"Come in," Indra called out. Pooja pushed the door open and stepped inside. Indra was seated on his usual seat at the desk; across from him sat a man, his back facing Pooja. As soon as she closed the door, he turned to look at her. Pooja stared at his face. He had strong, sharp features, a well-tamed moustache flowing into a rugged beard, thick eyebrows, and mysterious dark eyes, black as the sky on a moonless night. He would have been handsome and awe-inspiring if not for the scars slashed across his face. He looked like he had been in a dogfight where the mutts were crazy and half-starved to death. Now, he looked terrifying, assessing Pooja, waiting for her reaction. Truth be told, Pooja wanted to bolt; his face told many stories, all of them dark and horrible, but she couldn't run like a coward, especially now. She stepped closer to the man and waved.

"Hi, you must be Ramesh Patel. I am Pooja Bahl; it's nice to finally meet you," her voice was strong, unwavering. Pooja gave herself a mental pat on the back.

Ramesh smiled, the scars on his face stretched, making him look monstrous. "You are brave. I see that I scare you a lot."

"Your appearance does," Pooja admitted. "But a person is more than their appearance; a person is their personality, their soul. So far, you don't scare me. I've heard stories about you. Based on those, I feel like you are a brave soldier, loyal to the throne, so you interest me."

"I interest you," Ramesh repeated, his face void of emotion.

"Exactly," Pooja glanced at Indra, who was looking tense, his eyes flicking from Pooja to Ramesh and back again. Ramesh stood up; he was around six foot five inches, towering above everyone else, his muscles rippled as he pulled on his coat.

"I heard your speech; it was foolish of you to declare you would kill Prajwal with the little experience you have with weapons. I have read your assessments; you are doing well in your classes. You may even be the best, but it isn't enough."

"That's why I hope you would train me, sir," Pooja looked him dead in the eye, which was a little difficult for her as she was more than a foot shorter. "I don't intend to kill Prajwal, I intend to exorcise the ghost of his ancestor from inside him, and get him to our side. Prajwal is a formidable warrior, and we could really use him."

"Indra, it looks like you didn't tell me anything about Pooja," he stared at Indra who slowly got up. Pooja thought he was tall and composed, but standing before Ramesh, he looked small, weak even.

"I don't know her that well," Indra admitted. "Though I expected her to be more respectful."

Pooja hung her head; he was right, she should have kept her mouth shut. She might have ruined the one chance she had of fixing this mess.

"Respectful?" Ramesh shook his head. "You misunderstand me. Pooja has the spirit, she has the willpower, and she knows her goal. I understand Prajwal was responsible for the death of one of her loved ones, yet she put her personal differences aside so that she can do the right thing. She puts the safety of the world above her personal agendas, which most people are too selfish to do. You understand that, don't you? People talk about many things; rarely do they mean them. Pooja has what it takes. For now, let's see if my training will nurture the willpower or break her."

"Nurture, hopefully. Breaking sounds painful," Pooja mumbled. Ramesh turned to look at her with a hint of a smile on his face.

"Thank you for agreeing to train me," she added.

Ramesh nodded, "Pack your things and meet me near the gate in half an hour. Get your winged horse as well." Without saying anything, he exited the room.

"Is he always this mysterious?" Pooja wondered out loud.

"He is usually more terrifying. He smiled; did you see that? I never saw him smile before, and I have known him for more than twenty years."

"Maybe you weren't funny enough," Pooja shrugged.

"You impressed him."

"You sound surprised."

"I am, it usually takes Ramesh a long time to decide whether he wants to train someone or not."

"The future of the world literally depends on his decision, which obviously influenced him."

"No, you don't know Ramesh. He doesn't care about anything when it comes to training, which is totally justifiable. His training is..."

"Vigorous, not many can handle it. I know all this. I'd better go and pack."

"Yeah," Indra was staring at the seat opposite his, as though still unable to believe what had happened.

Not wanting to waste any more time, Pooja went to her room and threw some toiletries into a bag she found waiting for her on the bed. She put in her pajamas and a picture of Thalia, Anaaya, and herself, all eight years of age, holding ice cream and grinning at the camera without a worry in the world. She twirled around the room one last time, checking to see if she had missed something, and then went out, the door locking automatically as she shut it. She checked the time; her half-hour was almost up. She wanted to meet Arjun and Avi, but she didn't have the time. Her heart heavy with sadness that they hadn't bothered to come to say goodbye, she ran to the stables. She went to Shadow to find Arjun and Avi preparing him for the journey. He had been recently groomed, and they were wrestling him into a harness that was accompanied by pouches to hold weapons in case of an attack.

"Hey guys," Pooja ran toward them, grinning widely.

"Hey!" they yelled back as Pooja reached there and flung herself onto them. They held each other, smiling wildly for a while, and then pulled away.

"We came to say goodbye. We thought this would be the best place to do it," Avi smiled.

"I thought you wouldn't show up," Pooja admitted.

"Why would you think that?" Arjun frowned.

"You weren't near my room, and I guess most of the time people I care about don't care about me. I thought this was the same."

Avi reached forward and lightly slapped the back of her head, "Don't think that, stupid. We care about you and love you, right Arjun?"

Arjun cleared his throat. "Yes, of course."

"Aw, I love you guys too!" They hugged again.

"You'll be late. Here, climb on," Arjun helped her up onto her horse. As she settled herself on it, Arjun and Avi placed all the weapons in the pouches.

"Hey, good luck," Arjun said, swallowing hard.

"I have to use the washroom. I love you, bye, Pooja," Avi flashed a quick smile and left.

Arjun stared at her for a moment, "Bye now, I guess."

"Yeah, bye. Have fun when I'm gone. Don't forget to ask around. Say bye to your girlfriend as well; she was jealous of us the whole time. Tell her she doesn't need to worry about competition," Pooja laughed; it sounded hollow.

"Naina and I broke up a few weeks after term started," Arjun clarified. "So, I can't do that."

"Oh, I had no idea. Why?"

"It was because you came into my life, and I just knew I couldn't do justice to Naina."

"What do you mean by that?" Pooja's throat had gone dry.

"You are smart," Arjun smiled sadly. "You'll figure it out. You are getting late, bye."

"Bye, Arjun," Pooja flicked the reins, and Shadow galloped toward the gate, taking the same path, they took a few hours ago. Arjun's words played over and over in her head the whole time. By the time she reached Ramesh, she understood and couldn't stop smiling.

"Ready?" he asked.

"Ready," Pooja looked back once again, imagining Arjun's silhouette watching them ride out of the castle into the world Pooja once called home.

GUESS WHO DID NOT GET LOST IN THE WOODS

Ramesh and Pooja rode on for hours in the same forest Pooja, Mahi, and Ahan did in complete silence. Pooja didn't mind it; she had nothing to talk about anyway, and she was too interested in her surroundings to think about anything else. They took a different path this time, and a few hours later, the forest's surroundings changed completely. Instead of beautiful, lush green trees and bushes, some trees had soft lilac leaves, some glowed in the color, others were in similar shades. Pooja exhaled in wonder; the more she stared at the trees, the more details she noticed. It was like she stepped into a fairytale. The sun began to set, casting a warm glow, as Ramesh and Pooja rode.

"Won't we collect wood for fires and cooking?" Pooja finally asked as Ramesh gave no signs of stopping, even though the sun was setting. He didn't answer and rode on. Pooja sighed but followed him anyway. The sun set completely, and the forest was engulfed in darkness with wisps of violet light emitted from the trees. This path, too, was extremely silent with no signs of wildlife.

Ramesh stopped his horse at a small clearing. He tied the horse to a tree and instructed Pooja to do the same. She did and stretched her legs, grateful to be off the horse. Ramesh sat on the forest floor and slung a pack off his shoulder. It was camouflaged so perfectly that Pooja didn't even realize it was there. He took out two cans of beans, two spoons, and two bottles of water. Pooja sat across from him as he handed her share. Pooja gladly swallowed the beans as Ramesh slowly munched his. Pooja watched him as his eyes darted from tree to tree, looking for threats. When he was satisfied, he turned to Pooja.

"How are the beans?" he asked.

"They taste like beans," Pooja replied, feeling stupid.

"Okay," Ramesh cleared his throat.

They stared at each other for a while.

"So, where are we going?" Pooja asked, hoping to spark a conversation.

"My house," he swallowed.

"Are there any other kids there whom you are training?" Pooja inquired, hoping she didn't have to share a room with a million kids again.

"No, I wasn't training anybody for a long time now. You are the first after Mahi," he admitted.

"Do you live alone?" Pooja didn't want to live alone with him if his conversation skills were *this* bad.

"No, I live with my wife. She will tend to all your basic needs; all I will do is train you," he said, taking another bite of the tasteless beans. Pooja felt bad watching him eat this food.

"Do you have any children?" she asked, swallowing her skepticism.

Ramesh's eyes darkened dangerously, the night emphasizing the scars on his face. This was definitely a touchy topic. "No, as a matter of fact. I lost the ability to have kids the day Prajwal escaped the Base. I used to live in the quarters, and I stopped the asuras from invading the Base."

"Oh, I'm sorry," she winced.

"Why are you? You don't know me. Pooja, I don't need sympathy but brutal honesty." His eyes were harsh and unflinching, reflecting just how cruel the world was to him.

"Okay, I'll be honest with you," Pooja promised. "Do you want kids?"

"Of course I do, don't I look like I want them?" Ramesh glared at her as though he was going to skin her alive and eat roasted Pooja for dinner instead.

Pooja stared at him, shocked at the question. "No, you don't. You look like the scary dude who eats misbehaving children mothers tell their children about."

Ramesh smiled, "That's what I get for asking you to be brutally honest."

"Yeah, why haven't you considered adoption, then?" Pooja frowned; that was the obvious choice.

"First off, we didn't have the resources or mindsets to raise a child. Now that we do, we don't have the energy to raise a baby. We need a kid around your age, but it can't be *any* kid. To live in our house, as my child, you need to be able to withstand things that most people can't. The kid should not feel like an outsider, so he or she should be somewhat like us." Ramesh looked almost as surprised as Pooja felt, telling her so much about himself.

"Are you okay with me asking these questions?" Pooja wondered.

"Yes, they are better than mine anyway," he chuckled.

"True," she chuckled. "Why do people think you are scary or mean? You seem fine."

"I intimidate people, I don't like them getting close to me. Call it trust issues if you want; I push people away all the time. My wife had quite the challenge getting me to admit I loved her too, ask her sometime," he smiled. "I look like I can inspire fear, so I hold that image. This will give me respect, and my enemies will be scared of me. Fear will cloud your better judgment; I inspire fear so that my opponent will lose focus, hence I can win."

"So, your scary vibe is just a battle tactic?" Pooja asked, impressed.

"Almost everything I do is a battle tactic," Ramesh warned.

"What about telling me all these things about you?" Pooja toyed with her spoon.

"You will be living in my house. To adapt to my vigorous training schedule, you must first have a means of comfort, a place to feel like home. Home is just the people around you. My wife is naturally very homely, unlike me. I will try to make you feel comfortable however you need me to," he shrugged.

Pooja was impressed by how brutally analytical he was.

"Why didn't you be nice to Mahi?" she wondered suddenly.

"I was, she was a brilliant student," he tossed his empty can into the bushes.

"I mean, why doesn't she know anything about your life?" Pooja decided to ignore the littering.

"Nobody is brave enough to ask. I didn't push her or try to be friendly because she didn't need that from me." He assessed her for a second, "You do."

"Are you saying I don't have friends?" she tried to hide the bite in her tone.

"No," he shook his head. "I am saying you won't have many options to socialize at my house."

"When are we going to reach?" Pooja stretched, cracking her back.

"We will start again at first light, so we will reach by lunchtime. My wife is a great cook, you will see, it will be the best food you have eaten," his eyes warmed a bit, talking about his wife.

"I doubt that. I've eaten Arjun's food before; it tastes like it came from heaven. It's going to be pretty hard to beat that," Pooja didn't try to hide the skepticism.

"Yes, I ate his food before. Indra wanted me to train Arjun, but I found it unnecessary. He is a smart kid; he doesn't need more training than he has in the base. Indra made him cook to impress me," Ramesh raised an eyebrow, looking a bit like the Rock, but Indian and considerably hairier and maybe taller.

"What?" Pooja laughed, "Why would you be impressed by his cooking?"

"I know, right? It's not like I am looking for a wife," he chuckled. His voice was deep yet smooth, not monstrous at all. Pooja expected him to have a laugh like a bark, not sweet and so *normal*.

"Is your wife's anything like his?" she continued, hopeful as the conversation stretched.

"Yes, it is. Don't tell her I said this, but Arjun's is better."

"Definitely will tell her."

"Please don't," he groaned. Pooja smiled and rolled her eyes.

Ramesh got up and began to assemble a tent. He told Pooja to keep a lookout, and she did. It took him under two minutes to finish. Pooja turned; it looked exactly like the tent Ahan laid out for her not so long ago.

"Where are *you* going to sleep?" she asked, looking at the single tent standing in the corner of the clearing.

"I won't be sleeping. Who will keep a lookout?"

"I can call my guide; Simba will do it."

"No, I can't sleep anyway."

"Insomnia?"

"Yeah, since childhood. I couldn't sleep, so I focused on my powers, and look where it got me now."

"Oh, well, is there anything anyone can do?"

Ramesh shook his head. "This is the one battle I've lost multiple times. The battle in my head with the ghosts of my past."

Pooja nodded and retreated into her tent, leaving him to his thoughts. She lay down on her sleeping bag and stared at the top of the tent. Even though she had a long day and was physically exhausted, her brain was active. She thought of Ramesh; there was something about him that intrigued her. She knew that he wouldn't hurt her, but the fact that she was with Ramesh already meant that she was going to face Prajwal soon. She remembered the haunted look on his face as he realized how badly he had messed up, and she felt horrible for him. She wanted to help him, but she was still scared, terrified that she might not be able to do it. She wondered what would happen if she died; would the war never happen? Or was facing Prajwal the war, and she wasn't prepared? She shook her head, trying not to think about that without much success. She sighed and went out; Ramesh was pacing back and forth, sword in hand. His back was facing Pooja, but he turned as soon as Pooja came outside.

"What happened?" he asked.

"I can't sleep; can I guard with you?"

"How energetic are you right now?"

Pooja inhaled slowly, the night breeze ruffling her hair and clothes softly, her exhaustion cleared. She looked at Ramesh, "Pretty sure I won't sleep for a while."

"Are you ready to train, then?"

"Oh," Pooja was surprised. Training with Ramesh was supposed to be a big thing, and she wasn't prepared to do so until the day after. However, she wasn't sleepy and didn't want to waste time, so she agreed.

Ramesh asked her to show him how to do basic things like jabbing, dodging strikes, and disarming. He tested her knowledge about some moves theoretically. He asked her to show all the moves she had with various weapons such as the mace, the bow and arrow, and the lasso. It took her an hour to demonstrate everything she had been learning in the base. By the time she did, she was completely exhausted and collapsed on her sleeping bag.

She woke up in the morning, still a little exhausted, had more beans and set off west to Ramesh's house. In about an hour, Pooja fell asleep on Shadow and woke up again by mid-afternoon.

"How much longer?" she mumbled sleepily.

"We are almost here," Ramesh called back, and they turned left, coming face to face with a modest cottage. "Welcome home."

"You live in the middle of the jungle?"

"I know it's a little different from your luxury place at the palace, but you will have to make do."

"No, it's cool. It's like camping forever. It must be peaceful here, away from humans."

"Not quite. There is a small tribe that lives close by; they are good allies. They are a small community. We buy our food from them, and my wife stays with them when I leave for work."

"Work?"

"Yeah, Indra sends me to do some odd tasks whenever he needs it. I get paid quite a lot, and I still have money left from when I used to work in the base."

"There are people who live outside the base? Will they fight for us in the war?"

"They have a choice; these tribes can fight with either side, but they will choose us. The asuras are a lot worse than the devas; we are all well aware."

"Ramesh!" a woman stood at the door, clad in a simple peach cotton sari. She was smiling at the party. "And you must be Pooja. Welcome, dear. I am Vaishnavi, Ramesh's wife."

"Hi aunty," Pooja smiled and dismounted her horse.

"Call me Vaishnavi, dear. Ramesh, get ready, I'll serve you lunch. Pooja, I'll show you to your room, come on." She led her into the house, leaving Ramesh to lead Shadow to the stables. Their house looked like it came from a village setting. It had a chicken coop, stables for horses and cows, a well to draw water from, and a few plants at the entrance. Pooja followed Vaishnavi into the house, which had a huge living plus dining room that opened into a kitchen in the corner from which the smell of real food wafted through. There were three rooms in the house, the largest one being the Master Bedroom. Pooja was shown to the guest room, which was, like the whole house, made of mud. It had a small bed with faded sheets and a cooler. It had a small bathroom with a shower. She peeled the clothes off her body and got into it. She cleaned herself thoroughly, wrapped a towel around herself, and stepped out to see clothes laid out for her on the bed. She wore the shirt and tracks and went outside. Ramesh exited the Master Bedroom at the same time and greeted his wife with a hug.

"How have you been?" he murmured against her neck.

"Good, how about you? Did you sleep well last night?" she gently stroked his hair.

"No," he sighed, pressing his forehead to her shoulder. "I have a splitting headache, but you know I can't sleep without..." he stopped himself, noticing Pooja ogling at the two. He straightened quickly and held his wife's shoulders.

"Pooja," Vaishnavi nodded at her. "Come, let's eat. I made potato curry with pooris. I hope you like them."

"Yeah, it's one of my favourites," Pooja followed them into the kitchen.

They had the food quickly, with the couple exchanging a few words occasionally. Pooja inhaled the food; it was tasty. Not as much as Arjun's but close, just like Ramesh said. After Pooja finished her lunch, Ramesh informed her about the plan from now until six months later.

They would start her training the next day at first light. She would have to wake up early, help Vaishnavi around the house for a while, go out and warm up, train, eat, train some more, eat, and sleep. For the day, she could do whatever she wanted and explore the woods only accompanied by Simba, Vaishnavi, or Ramesh. Pooja nodded along, helped Vaishnavi wash the dishes, and crashed again. She woke up, went outside, and found the house empty. She tried opening the doors, found all of them locked, so she went outside through the back door. She knew instantly that this is where she was going to train. There was a small arena built over a small stretch of land that could be used for hand-to-hand combat, sword fighting, and more. She walked around the ground where she would spend most of her time and went back inside. Vaishnavi was tiptoeing out of the Master Bedroom, closing the door quietly.

She spotted Pooja walking in. "Hey, where were you?" she whispered.

"Out," Pooja whispered back, "I went back and saw the training arena."

"Many heroes were trained back there," she smiled proudly.

"Where is Ramesh uncle?"

"He's sleeping. It took a while, but he is. He'll probably scream; it's disturbing. Be quiet and don't worry about it, okay?"

"Sure, why does he have insomnia?"

"That's not my story to tell. He will tell you if he wants to."

"That's alright. This place seems pretty boring though. What do you do during the day?"

"Ramesh is a very interesting person, so usually spending time with him helps. When he is out or sleeping, I go to the tribe and spend time with the people there, and when I feel like staying at home, I read. Do you read?"

"Oh, yeah, a lot. I am an avid reader, actually. I have read over a thousand books."

"Amazing, I finished two thousand recently."

"Wow, how did you do that?"

"I have a lot of time on my hands," she chuckled. "I'll give you some books."

"My schedule is pretty packed; I don't think I can read."

"Yes, you can. Dinner is at seven pm, and early light is usually after five. You will have at least two hours per day to read."

"That's awesome."

An ear-splitting scream echoed from the master bedroom.

"No! Leave me!" Ramesh was howling, "No!"

Vaishnavi threw open the door and stepped inside. For a split second, Pooja could see Ramesh sprawled on the bed, clutching the sheets tight, his head thrown back, eyes scrunched, and mouth open in a terrible scream. Vaishnavi's pale face paled even more as she peered down at him with her almond-shaped chestnut eyes. Then, she looked up and pursed her lips in pain before shutting the door. The screams stopped, and whimpering took its place. She heard Ramesh's quiet sobs and the soothing murmuring of Vaishnavi. Pooja released a breath she didn't know she was holding and retreated to her room. She lay on the bed, looking at the ceiling. This became her favourite pose, thinking about her friends back at the Base but refusing to think about Ramesh. She wondered what he went through to be so deeply affected.

A few hours later, Vaishnavi walked in holding a couple of crime thriller novels and gave them to Pooja.

"I thought you would like these kinds of books."

"Yeah, I love crime thrillers, thanks."

Vaishnavi sat down next to Pooja. "Hey, about this afternoon. That can be really disturbing."

"You don't say," Pooja cracked her knuckles in nervousness. She tried to forget about that, but the screams shook her to the core.

"Yeah, this is one of the main reasons Ramesh doesn't let anyone close to him. Sometimes he loses control and it's scary. He had demons in his past that haunt him a lot even now. His life isn't sunshine and daisies either; he pretends he doesn't care but every human he kills leaves a scar on him. I wish I could help him, but he doesn't let me. I don't know what to do."

"Have you considered therapy?"

"Yeah, I did," she rubbed her temples. "He won't open up to anybody. I tried so hard, but he's just too intimidating. No therapist will risk it, you know? They all are terrified that he would break their bones or murder their families, and you know," she choked out a chuckle, "he just might."

An idea hit Pooja like a truck, "Hey, you said you have a lot of free time and you want to help your husband, right?"

"Yeah, obviously I want to help."

"Why don't you study psychology?"

"What do you mean?"

"Study and become a shrink yourself. You are not scared of your husband, are you?"

"I'm not. I can't believe I never thought of that. Thank you. Enjoy your books; dinner will be ready in ten minutes," Vaishnavi got up to leave.

"Do you need help?"

"No, cooking is a task I like to do alone. It's therapeutic."

"Have fun!"

"You too," she closed the door behind her as she left.

Pooja ate dinner in silence, not knowing what to say. Vaishnavi chatted, informing them about the latest gossip in the village. Pooja pretended to be interested in the scandalous love story between two young tribals. As soon as dinner was finished, Ramesh retired to the room he shares with his wife to prepare himself for the next day, leaving Pooja alone with Vaishnavi. The two of them cleared the dishes and washed them while Vaishnavi hummed a little tune to herself.

She turned to Pooja as both of them wiped their hands on a cloth.

"Thank you for not mentioning his nightmares during dinner."

"Why would I? I don't want to get beaten over dinner," Pooja laughed. "Never talk about anything serious during meals. It is disrespectful to the goddess of food, Annapurna Devi."

"Beaten? My husband won't ever lay a finger on you unless it is for training," Vaishnavi looked shocked.

"I mean, beating is part of gaining strength, right? So, you won't be weak anymore. Pain gives strength, that's what my parents say." Pooja looked at Vaishnavi's enraged face and realized that, maybe, she was saying something unusual. Something very wrong.

"Pooja, when you say 'beating,' what exactly do you mean? What did your parents do to you?" she asked carefully, placing the cloth on a marble countertop.

Pooja shrugged, unsure where this conversation was going. She thought she had made an offhand comment. "Well, nothing unusual. My dad used to hit me with a belt or call me out on my flaws so I could work on them."

"Call you out on your flaws?"

"Yeah. Like, if I cry about my bruises, he tells me I am being weak so next time, I cover up and bravely to not show my pain. Things like that."

Vaishnavi stepped forward and hugged Pooja. This hug felt comfortable, warm, and motherly. This was how she imagined hugging Mahi would feel, and now, this was how she wished her mom would hold her. "Oh gods, I am so sorry you had to go through all that."

"What do you mean?" Pooja pulled away. She understood. This wasn't normal either, this was considered abuse as well. She turned and walked away to her room. She shut the doors quietly and sank onto her bed. She got up, changed her clothes, and climbed under the covers. Only then, in the dark with the fan's constant movement blowing cold air onto her face, did she let her emotions seep through her from her eyes in the form of tears. She clutched the blanket close to her chest and sobbed quietly. She hated being different; she hated how her reality shifted every single day. She hated how she never fit in, never felt like she belonged. Not with Thalia and Anaaya, not with her fellow Yamas, not with Meher. Only with Arjun and Avi did she feel some sort of connection, that they could relate to some parts of her life. She was never truly herself with anybody. She didn't know who she was herself. Not the princess, not the abused poor child, not the quirky student. She was none of these things; she was something else. Something different. She had to fit in.

"You don't have to fit in," a voice spoke in her head. A soft, feminine voice, a motherly one. Caring. "You are different, and that is the best thing about you." Her heart began to beat regularly again, her tears stopped flowing, she drifted into a dreamless sleep.

TRAINING WITH RAMESH

Pooja was woken up at the crack of dawn by Vaishnavi. She touched Pooja's arm, and that got her to wake, fully conscious.

"What?" she gasped in shock, scuttling away from her touch.

"Good morning, time for your lessons. Get dressed and go outside," Vaishnavi indicated the clothes lying on the desk in the far corner of the room Pooja hadn't noticed the previous night. She stayed motionless until Vaishnavi left, closing the doors behind her. Pooja took out her toothbrush from her bag and went to the washroom, grabbing the clothes. She stepped out dressed in an athletic black shirt and yoga pants, clinging to her thin frame. She tied her waves in a high ponytail and went outside.

Ramesh was standing there, dressed in a sleeveless shirt that exposed his bulging muscles, each bigger than Pooja's face. His well-built body was visible through the tight fabric. Tattoos peeked out from his shoulders, leading into the shirt. He looked up and down at Pooja and shook his head.

"You don't look like much, we have to fix that," he commented. That's it, no 'good morning,' no 'how did you sleep last night?' This was the Ramesh that scared the hell out of people, who trained heroes to be the best version of themselves. By being scary.

"What do you mean? I can fight," Pooja crossed her arms and glared at him. At her above-average height of five foot three, she felt tiny in front of him.

"The way you hold your body affects your performance in a fight. You must intimidate your enemy; you must show confidence. It is hard to do so when you are built like a stick."

Pooja turned red in embarrassment. She was never conscious of her lanky figure before, but she wanted to cover up. Goosebumps erupted on her hands and face as she cowered away from Ramesh.

"Let's start training," Ramesh said, "Run five laps around the perimeter."

After running, there was stretching. After that, there was sword fighting, where she duelled with Ramesh and lost miserably.

"Watch my sword, move to defend yourself, stop following a pattern. This is not a written exam; your moves should block mine. Your enemy won't fight according to the techniques you have learnt in school," Ramesh kept repeating. By the end of the sword fighting lesson, she was battered and bruised. Pooja was drenched in sweat, panting, and they took a break where Pooja gulped down water.

They did archery next, where Pooja shot bullseye after bullseye. She had taken up archery as an extracurricular activity to spend time away from home. Ramesh was not impressed.

"You take too much time. We will do moving targets tomorrow; your enemy won't wait for you to load an arrow, aim, and then shoot. He will shoot, and you will die."

"Real optimistic," Pooja muttered.

Annoyance flashed in Ramesh's eyes. "Optimism will not save your life, take it from me. Don't be in a bubble of denial if you are expecting to win this fight."

"Alright, I am sorry. I will aim better next time."

"That I am sure of," a flicker of a smile emerged on Ramesh's face. That was a good sign.

After a quick lunch of protein and more protein, Pooja and Ramesh continued the training.

As Prajwal could read and control minds up to a certain point, Pooja spent the next few hours learning human psychology techniques and tried to recall the ways a person can be manipulated.

"Do you think you will fall for silly psychology tricks? Like they do at parties for little kids?" Ramesh asked suddenly.

"What, like, guessing the number I picked or something?" Pooja asked, bemused. "Of course not."

"Say silk twenty times," Ramesh instructed. Pooja carried out the command, feeling extremely confused.

"What do cows drink?" Ramesh asked.

"Milk," Pooja replied. "Wait, no, they don't. They drink water."

Ramesh laughed, "You can't control your reactions to something as simple as this. How will you stand up against Prajwal? You have to work harder."

Pooja did not disappoint. For the next six months, she pushed herself harder than she ever had. She dedicated her entire day to the training, without any distractions. She didn't hear from anyone back at the Base, as she told Ramesh she didn't need the distractions. She refrained from thinking about her old life and started the training as a new chapter in her life.

One night Pooja dreamt of her father. This was the earliest memory she had of him. The day he began to hit her. Pooja was four, and she had just finished a drawing, which she was proud of. It was of her, her parents, and a small cat. She went to her father's study to show it to him. He was on a call and was agitated.

"Dad? Dad?" Pooja called.

"What?" he snapped.

"Look, it's us in a big castle. You are the king, mom the queen, and I am the princess."

Her father took the drawing and ripped it. "I'm not a king; you aren't a princess. You're a nobody."

"No, I'm not. I'm a princess and I have powers, just like Rapunzel."

Jayanth's eyes widened in rage; he reeked of alcohol. "Powers? You're powerless, weak, and pathetic!" He brought his hand down sharply, and Pooja felt her cheek sting in pain. Her father did not stop even when she began to cry and beg.

The dream shifted to Thalia's death. As the arrow pierced her, she heard her father's voice, "Powerless, weak, and pathetic."

She woke up with a start, panting, her face covered in tears and sweat.

"It's okay, it's okay," Ramesh was rocking her as she sobbed into his arms. "You showed me your dream, I saw what he did."

Pooja buried her face in embarrassment. Transferring thoughts and images was also a minor power she began to learn, but clearly could not control.

"You are so brave for dealing with all that on your own. So brave," he made her look him in the eye. "You aren't powerless, weak, or pathetic. He is. He hit his daughter because he couldn't deal with his past. He is unworthy of having you as his child. That man brings shame to mankind as a whole."

Pooja sobbed again, his words enveloping her in a comfortable warmth. "Thank you."

"Don't thank me. I just wished someone was there for me. You remind me of me when I was younger," he shook his head and smiled. "We'll go to the village tomorrow. No studies. We'll just go and take a break. Just you, me, and Vaishu, okay?"

"Alright."

The next day, the three of them went to the small village on their steeds. They bought stuff for the house, some wooden swords for training as the previous ones broke, and had lunch. Vaishnavi took Pooja shopping, and they bought clothes. Ramesh introduced them to the village head, whom he was close with. He wore a dhoti with a third eye tattooed on his forehead. They worshipped Mahakali, the goddess of destruction.

He assessed Pooja, "Is she your daughter, Ramesh?"

Ramesh smiled genuinely, "Yes."

Pooja's heart could have exploded with joy. They went back to the cottage and never spoke of that again.

After what seemed like an eternity, the six months of training with Ramesh began to come to an end. One day, as Pooja was sitting in her room, she heard a knock on her door.

"Come in," she said, not looking up from the book of duelling techniques Ramesh had given her.

The door creaked open as Ramesh stepped into the room. Pooja knew it was him from the slight sound of his heavy footsteps. She heard him lean against the door; she knew his arms were crossed. He always crossed his arms before talking about something important. She looked up from her book.

"We need to talk. You, me, and my wife. Come to the living room," he said, then turned and left. She sighed as she shut her book, placing it on her desk cluttered with murder mystery novels and books on warfare techniques.

Vaishnavi and Ramesh sat on the floor next to each other, arms softly brushing against each other. Vaishnavi's doe eyes were alight with the kind of happiness one gets with a loved one. Pooja suppressed a smile and sat opposite them.

"What?" she asked, skipping the small talk. She really wanted to get back to her book.

"As you know, your training time is ending," Ramesh began, "So, I wanted to give you something." He produced a Rudraksh. "This was given to me by Lord Karthikeya. He visited me once and gave me this Rudraksh. He told me that his father, Mahadev, wanted me to have it. It protects the wearer from death once. It looks like you will have more use for it than me." He fastened it around her neck,

"Thank you so much for this. I know how much this Rudraksh means to you, especially if Lord Shiva gave it. Will I meet gods too?"

"Only if they deem it necessary." He cleared his throat. "Now we have to talk about what you will do with Prajwal."

"I have some ideas," Pooja's free time was occupied with thoughts of defeating Prajwal.

"I would love to hear them, and so would the rest of our companions."

"Companions? The horses?" Pooja snorted.

Vaishnavi smiled, her soft features seemingly smiling with her. "No, not the horses. King Indra, the queen, and the princes are arriving tomorrow to discuss your progress as well as the future plans."

"They are coming *tomorrow*?" Pooja asked, alarmed. Her thoughts went to blue eyes, soft smiles, and the smell of the ocean breeze.

"Yeah, aren't you excited?" Vaishnavi laughed softly.

"Well, I mean, yes. No. I don't know. So many things have changed about me, will they even recognize me?"

"They sent you here so that you can change for the better, Pooja," Ramesh frowned. "What are you worried about, they won't reject you. You are the best student I have had so far."

Pooja blushed. Ramesh never gave out compliments lightly, and she never heard them back at home. She was glad to know her hard work paid off. Yet, she couldn't keep herself from nervously twisting her ring. Her grandfather's ring, they discovered, could turn into more than one type of weapon when she touched it. She had to be extra careful and not think about weapons while brushing against it, or the ring would expand into the weapon in her head.

"Are you worried about Arjun's reaction once he sees you?" Vaishnavi asked with a knowing look in her eyes.

Pooja turned red with embarrassment, "No."

"Yeah right," Vaishnavi scoffed. "Don't worry, I understand your dilemma. When I was younger, I used to be awkward in front of Ramesh, embarrassing myself to get his attention. He never gave me any, and when he went off to higher-order training to control souls, I decided to grow up. I became an independent woman, strong. When Ramesh came back and saw me three years later, I was no longer the awkward, giggly teenager in love. He went behind me to win my heart; he noticed me when I became myself. Stepping up into who you were meant to be will be good for you."

Pooja let her shoulders relax. She nodded. "Is that it?"

"No, we will practice controlling human souls," Ramesh announced.

"Human souls?" Pooja and Ramesh started Yama-based training after a week of physical and mental training. They practiced with insect souls and moved on to animal ones. This was the first time she was going to control a human. Controlling humans didn't sound right to Pooja, but she had to.

"Yes. We have to show the king that you are capable tomorrow. I think you are ready as well."

"Who do I practice on? What do I do?"

"You ask too many questions. How many times have I told you that?" Ramesh sighed.

"Fifty-four times. As you said, and I quote, 'Curiosity is good. Asking questions is better. Ask me things.'" Pooja tilted her head, hands laced together, elbows resting on her legs, and chin on hands.

Ramesh sighed and smiled, "You will be practicing on me. You will have to wrench my soul from my body and then put it back inside."

"What?" Pooja and Vaishnavi exclaimed at the same time.

"Did you not hear what I just said?" Ramesh asked curtly.

"No way in hell are you going to do that to yourself," Vaishnavi's voice turned stern.

"Vaishu…"

"No, don't Vaishu me. You will not put yourself in danger like that."

"Don't you trust Pooja on this?"

"No!" Vaishnavi hesitated before turning to Pooja, "No offense."

"None taken. I don't trust myself. I will kill you. Even if I manage to get the soul out of your body, which, by the way, gets tougher as the organism gets bigger. Putting it back is super risky. I don't want you to become the rabbit."

Once, while Pooja was practicing on a rabbit, she accidentally sent its soul to a plant nearby and didn't find it since then. They had rabbit stew for dinner but it felt wrong. It was quite literally soulless.

"I won't become the rabbit. That was your first and only failure. I trust you; you trust yourself."

"No."

"It's a direct order."

Pooja growled. Ramesh made it very clear that if she disobeyed a direct order from him, all her memories of training would be erased permanently. This was a precaution to ensure that Ramesh's students wouldn't betray him.

"Fine, but if your husband dies, swear not to cook me for lunch?" Pooja asked Vaishnavi.

"Don't worry, if he dies, I will cook him for lunch."

Ramesh laughed, "I love my bloodthirsty, cannibalistic wife."

"You have lost your mind."

"I can't think straight when I'm around you," he smiled and leaned closer to her.

Curling her lip in disgust, Pooja interrupted, "Does that mean that you gave the direct order when you were not in your right mind?" She could disobey those.

"You ruined the moment, you know?" Ramesh sighed. "And don't even think about disobeying that order."

Pooja scoffed and went back into her room. She sighed and rubbed her knuckles on her temple. She pulled away a cloth that covered the mirror. A cloth she draped the second day of her training session. She hadn't looked at her reflection since then. As the cloth slid down, she gasped.

Pooja grew a couple of inches taller; her back was stiffer; she held herself with more confidence. Her arms were no longer stick-thin; instead, they had muscles, not too much, but enough to flex. Her legs did not look like they were going to give away anymore. Instead, they were strong, powerful enough to deliver kicks that could knock people out. Her brown eyes were wide in shock, but the light in them was different. It was powerful, almost cruel. There was a scar slashed across her left eyebrow. Her worry lines were gone, and her face was fully sharp. She looked, felt, and was a warrior. She smiled, the moment making her face look beautiful. She moved back and, unable to resist, pulled out her sketchbook from under her bed. It was a muted red bound book with thick papers.

She made drawings to calm herself throughout these months. She flipped to the pages where she drew herself with Meher, with Avi, with Arjun. She brushed her fingers on the paper and smiled softly. She *was* looking forward to seeing them.

Pooja changed into a casual dhoti and blouse and strapped on her armor. Ramesh insisted that she wear traditional clothes during power training, claiming that they ensure maximum connection to the God and the power. She wrapped an *angavastram* around her shoulders. Pooja and Ramesh found out that her powers worked best in traditional attire; it was something about connecting with nature in the best possible way. She put on her sandals and walked outside, hearing soft clatters in her training ground. She went outside and saw Ramesh and Vaishnavi pushing all the equipment aside. She sipped some water from her bottle which she left on a table that morning. She stood opposite Ramesh and wiped the sweat off her brow. Vaishnavi stood on her toes and planted a soft kiss on his cheek and stood in the middle of the cluster of furniture.

"Are you ready?" Ramesh asked.

"No," Pooja admitted, feeling a little lightheaded.

"Focus on my soul. Take your own time."

Pooja closed her eyes, took a deep breath, and stretched out her arm, searching for the soul. She felt the concentrated energy in multiple places; one within herself, one opposite her, one near the cluster, and some near the trees. The tree spirits were weaker and gentler. She focused on the one opposite her, blocking everything else. She felt the energy pulsating under her palm. She felt the energy stretch, reaching out to her just as she was. She closed her palm; the energy was under her control now. She pulled it closer to her, feeling the energy come closer. She heard screams and sobs, but they were distant. She opened her eyes and saw a flicker, which she focused on. It began to glow brighter; she forced it to go back to the fallen form of her teacher and lowered it to his heart. The energy seeped into him, and he woke up with a start.

Ramesh forced himself onto his elbows, "Good job, kid." His eyes rolled up into his skull, and he fell back down. Vaishnavi rushed toward him, her eyes red and swollen. She had been crying. She dabbed Ramesh's head with a cool cloth and trickled some *amrutham*, the drink of the gods, into his mouth. Diluted *amrutham* helped the healing process of the blessed, giving them a burst of energy, though it didn't make them immortal. A stream flowed through the heavens onto a few places on Earth, which was a mixture of *amrutham* and the water from River Ganga, said to originate from Lord Shiva's bun itself. Remaking the diluted *amrutham* was not possible. Ramesh coughed, but his eyes stayed closed. Vaishnavi pressed her ear onto his chest.

"His pulse is stronger; he will be all right by morning," she announced softly, taking his right hand in hers and bringing it to her face.

Pooja wanted to say something. She wanted to move closer, but she collapsed out of sheer exhaustion.

POOJA'S UNOFFICIAL GRADUATION

When Pooja woke up, she couldn't open her eyes. She was aware of her surroundings and she could feel each part of her body, the way her chest rose and fell, and the way her heart beat evenly. She could smell the strong scent of scented candles essential in the healing process, feel the cool cloth pressed against her forehead, and hear distinct voices muttering. She couldn't make out what was being said or who the voices belonged to, so she tried to open her eyes yet again, but it felt like someone was physically not letting her move.

"Pooja, are you awake?" Vaishnavi's soft voice whispered in her ear, "The king and the princes have arrived."

Pooja's eyes snapped open successfully. "What happened?" she mumbled groggily.

Vaishnavi jumped back, startled by the sudden movement. "You collapsed and slept like a log for almost twelve hours. My husband is outside, sharing your progress with our guests. They want to meet you; the princes are eager, especially Arjun." She winked.

Pooja regretted sharing her feelings toward Arjun with Vaishnavi. She rolled her eyes and sat up, her body sore. Vaishnavi left as Pooja changed into a loose shirt and pants. She gulped down some water placed on her desk and went outside, patting her hair down.

She saw the king, looking exactly like the first time she saw him, outfit included. The only difference was that he had discarded the cape at the entrance to reveal himself dressed in a crisp suit. Avi wore a green suit, complementing his eyes. Arjun, however, wore a gray t-shirt and black joggers; he looked like a normal teenager. He had grown out his hair, which was now messed up, a few locks falling into his eyes, light stubble indicated his entrance into puberty. He sat casually, draping his right arm across the couch, his eyes were fixed on her, taking her in just as she was taking him in. When their eyes met, he gave her a soft smile which she returned. She felt Avi's gaze on her and turned to see him smiling sneakily at her and making kissing faces indicating her and Arjun. She frowned at him and stood behind Ramesh, noticing how Avi looked a couple of inches taller and more muscular than his brother. She didn't see the queen anywhere.

"Hello Pooja, we were just talking about you," Indra smiled.

"Good morning," she replied.

"We heard what happened yesterday with Ramesh and I have to say, I am impressed with your progress."

"Did you also hear the part where I collapsed and woke up just now?"

"Well, yes. That is why we have made certain adjustments to the plan," Indra said, sitting forward and fixing his eyes on Pooja. "We all have noticed the chemistry between you and Arjun," he began. Pooja blushed and glanced at Arjun, who was covering his laughter with his hand.

"We believe that Arjun is the prince," Indra continued.

"Surprise, surprise," Avi snorted.

Indra frowned at his son and continued, "So, we will send Arjun with you and Sharanya as backup to create the whole 'the two brave lovers successfully destroyed the looming threat of Prajwal before ascending the throne' story."

"What if we fail to do so?" Pooja wondered.

"Optimistic as always," Indra said dryly, "Then your life will go down as a tragic love story and we all die."

"Alright, so there isn't much of an option to fail."

"There never was."

"Anyways, Pooja, gather your things and we will send you off," Ramesh stood up.

"Wait, how are you?" Pooja asked.

"I'm okay now. I woke up before you and had time to adjust."

"What about breakfast?"

Ramesh rubbed his face in frustration. "You know, you are annoying. I am glad you will leave today."

"Really?" Pooja tried to keep the disappointment out of her voice. During these six months, she began to see Ramesh as a father figure, and he treated her like a daughter more than her father ever had. She didn't realize how close she had become with him in such a short period of time.

"Of course not," Ramesh placed a hand on Pooja's shoulder. "You can contact me whenever you want. Send a messenger pigeon."

"Why can't we just text?"

"Texts can be intercepted. I remember mentioning this before, but messenger birds are protected by the god of messengers and fire, Agni dev."

"Breakfast," Pooja repeated.

Arjun chuckled softly.

They had breakfast. Pooja sat between Arjun and Avi. She kept trying to talk to the former, but the latter would not shut up.

"So, what cool things can you do?" Avi demanded.

"You are such a child," Pooja rolled her eyes at the tone of his voice. She began to explain what she had learnt while eating uthappam with peanut chutney, just to notice Avi was pretending to fall asleep. She whacked him on the head with her left hand.

"What? It was so boring," Avi smiled.

"It wasn't boring," Arjun looked at her. She looked back with a smile.

"Thank you. See, smart people find that interesting," she told Avi.

"Not smart people, people who are in love with you and who don't want to seem that way. People who couldn't stop talking about you in the chariot but aren't talking to you to keep the 'I don't care' attitude," Avi corrected.

Pooja and Arjun blushed.

"I hate you," Arjun muttered.

"I heard you," Pooja informed, giving him a teasing smile. "Couldn't stop talking about me, huh? What did you say?"

They spent the whole breakfast teasing Arjun while the grown-ups spoke about depressing topics such as politics, war, and Prajwal.

After the meal was complete, Indra turned to Pooja, interrupting Avi's monologue about how Loki, from the Marvel Franchise, was the most misunderstood villain.

"So, Pooja, I've heard a detailed report on your progress over the past six months. Not surprisingly, you have done very well. You are physically as well as mentally capable of controlling a soul. If you can manage that at such a tender age with only six months of practice, I can only imagine all the great things you will do in your life, Princess."

"Your Highness..." Pooja was cut off.

"Oh, I am no longer the acting king. Arjun's lessons have just completed, as have yours. He will be crowned the King and you the Queen as soon as you both return with Prajwal. Also, with the existence of a Princess, there is no requirement for me."

It was true that along with studying her ability, she had to cram politics into her head. She could memorize most of it, but she didn't enjoy it as much as she enjoyed war tactics. She had to get used to it soon if politics would be a large part of her life. However, Pooja also caught the suppressed sadness in Indra's voice.

"There is still a requirement for you. Arjun, Avi, and I, we all need you. We will mess up multiple times in the future, I'm sure, and we will look to you for guidance."

Indra smiled softly, "I know you kids, you always try to find the answer on your own."

"Yes," Pooja agreed, "but in the end, we always turn to you."

Indra smiled again.

"We are going a little off-topic," Ramesh interrupted. "Pooja, Indra wants you to demonstrate your powers."

"On you?"

"That will not be required. We have a rabbit this time. You have to travel back to the Base on a horse, and we don't want to drag you unconscious. It won't be the greatest impression on its citizens."

"Was that a joke?" Pooja gasped in mock surprise.

Ramesh smiled one of his rare smiles and led the group to the practice grounds.

"Cool!" Avi exclaimed, "The grounds are huge. I bet I can't run a lap without getting exhausted."

"What do you mean?" Pooja snorted, "I can run three. I do it every day."

Avi looked dumbstruck, and Pooja had to smile. She missed getting into silly quarrels with Avi.

"I bet I could do one lap without falling flat on my face," Arjun laughed.

"Wanna race?" Avi demanded.

"Sure, be the referee, Poo," he gestured at Pooja.

"Call me that one more time and I will get a ghost to haunt you," she snapped.

"Geez, countdown," Avi pumped his fists in the air and began to warm up. Arjun crouched down and got into position.

"Three, two, one!" Pooja yelled as the boys began to sprint.

Pooja turned to see Ramesh holding a rabbit, while Indra and Vaishnavi stood at the entrance, watching them.

Ramesh let go of the rabbit, which took off. Pooja imagined skeletal bones emerging from the ground and creating a barrier in front of the rabbit, then its back. Soon it was surrounded on all sides, trapped in a skeletal cage, shrieking in fear.

"It's gonna be okay," Pooja called out. She focused on the soul; the energy wasn't as strong as Ramesh's, but she could feel the energy. She pulled it toward her, willing it to leave the rabbit. She heard a terrified squeak as the soul left the rabbit. Immediately she lowered it into the rabbit, which jerked back to life. Pooja let the ground absorb the bones and fell to her knees in exhaustion. Apart from fatigue and a splitting headache, she was feeling alright. When Vaishnavi handed her a glass of diluted *amrutham*, she gulped it down and instantly felt better.

"Whoa," Avi muttered in awe.

"That was some really dark magic," Arjun exhaled.

"I can do that to humans too," she threatened. She meant it as a joke, but when she saw the fear in Avi's eyes, she realized how spooked they might be feeling. Watching a soul leave a living thing naturally wasn't pretty, but to be forced out of it? It must have been terrifying.

"But I would probably die with you guys," she added. "You guys are the best, I love you, and I can't live without you."

Avi smiled, mischief replacing the fear in his eyes. "Arjun's got competition, I guess."

Pooja rolled her eyes at him and looked at Indra, who was immersed in a conversation with Ramesh yet again.

"Are you packed?" Arjun asked suddenly.

"Yeah, why?" Pooja replied.

"Why don't I help you load your luggage onto Shadow?"

"You brought Shadow?" Pooja exclaimed; she loved that horse.

"Yeah, he was really looking forward to meeting you. You are really good with animals; how do you do that?" Avi asked.

"You just show them love."

"Where are your bags, let me get them," Avi began to move toward the door. Pooja's shoulders slumped; she wanted to spend some time alone with Arjun. Before she could do anything, Arjun grabbed Avi's arm. He turned around and both the boys looked at one another. After a second, Avi's eyes widened.

"Or, I could stay here and eavesdrop on the elder's conversations." He walked toward his father, but not before bumping into Pooja and whispering, "I want details. All of them."

Pooja ignored him as Arjun approached her, and they went to her room. As Arjun grabbed her backpack, she pulled out her sketchbook from under the mattress.

"What's that?" he asked her, tracing his finger on the cover page.

"Just a few sketches I made."

"Can I see?"

Pooja looked back, realizing how close they were. She could see the shades of blue of his eyes and count the eyelashes on each of his eyes. He was slightly taller than her when she left the Base, but now he was nearly two meters in height, towering over her, even though she was almost 5'8.

"All right," she handed him the book.

Arjun unslung her backpack and plopped himself on the bed. Pooja sat next to him as he skimmed through the pages. There were illustrations of animals, the training grounds, the Base, her room, Thalia and Anaaya, Meher, and a lot of the royal family. There were a few sketches of her parents, but they were more personal.

In the one Arjun was looking at, her mother, portrayed as a weakling, was pressed against the wall. She was bony, her hair looked thin, with tears flowing out of her fearful eyes. She held a hand up as though defending herself. Her father looked like a giant next to her mother. He had a tail and horns, like the devil. His mouth was open in mid-scream, his face scrunched in anger, his eyes blazing with cold fury. In one hand he held a leather whip and in the other a bottle of poison. He was brandishing the whip at her mother. Pooja sat on her knees, shielding her mother as much as she could with her body. Even though she looked brave, her expression betrayed her, showing the terror she was hiding.

Arjun traced Pooja's face and looked up at her. She stared at the picture. She drew it a couple of months prior. That day Ramesh told the village chief she was his daughter. Pooja could finally think of her parents without any pain. She was disconnected from them, happier with Ramesh and Vaishnavi. They let her go on rides and bought her presents. She felt like she was a part of a real family that day. She wanted to hug them both and fall asleep, but she retreated to her bedroom instead. She thought about her family that night and drew the picture in the sketchbook.

"What is this?" Arjun's voice was filled with fury.

Pooja told him about her family. About how her father used to physically beat her and her mother and torture them. How she had to put on a straight face and pretend everything was alright in school and in front of her friends. How her family pretended to be perfect at functions, while at home they were a mess. How she went into severe depression and tried to end things multiple times, but couldn't stomach it every time. She told him how when she was about to make a drastic, emotional decision, she felt the roar of a tiger reverberate through her, calming her down. She now realized it was Simba protecting her from afar.

She told him about opening up to Mahi in the seventh grade, who advised her that it would help to see Mahi's therapist. She told him how she stole money from her dad's storage and went to her first therapy session. She told him about how she had lied and said her dad dropped her off before leaving. Even in therapy, she was not able to fully open up for fear that social services would come knocking on her door and expose her father. She explained how afraid she was of what her father would do if he found out she had been sharing things about her life with a stranger. She felt that she couldn't even go to Mahi for help and found herself pretending that everything was okay in front of her, her friends, and the therapist. How she pretended so much that she herself believed she was overreacting to the situation. She soon quit therapy once her therapist had given her the all-clear. She had managed to fool everyone but had never really healed from the scars given by her father, both physical and mental.

Pooja stopped twisting the bedsheet and looked up at Arjun. His eyes were brimming with tears.

He took a deep breath. "I don't know what to say," he said. His voice cracked. He put the sketchbook aside, moved forward, and placed his arm on her shoulder.

"Is that why you move away when someone initiates contact with you? Because you are afraid that we are trying to hurt you?"

Pooja nodded, feeling the tears pricking her eyes.

"But you always hug and cuddle, why is that?"

"If I swear off physical contact, people are going to think there is something wrong with me. I am bubbly and clingy so people don't think that. So that people think I am a normal, happy girl. Not a screw-up."

"You put so much thought into this."

"Yeah, after a beating, I was locked in my room for hours, sometimes days. That gave me a lot of time to think."

"Locked in your room?"

"Yeah, my father would take my mother to their room and lock me inside mine. He would refuse to unlock the door. I would tell my teacher I was unwell the next day when I went to school in case I missed it. I tried not to get him mad before the days I needed to go to school, whether it was for exams or school plays and stuff like that."

"Why didn't you tell me before?"

"I wasn't ready. I knew I had to trust you completely. This is my biggest secret. Apart from me, and now you, nobody knows. People I've told only know it in bits and pieces. You know the full story."

"You trust me completely now?"

"I am putting my life in your hands willingly, Arjun. Of course, I trust you."

"Why?" his voice was hoarse now.

"I don't know," Pooja's voice broke. "I can look into your eyes and tell that you won't betray me. Ever."

Arjun sighed, cupping Pooja's face. He leaned forward and engulfed her in a hug. Wrapping his arms around her and pulling her into his warm embrace. She rested her head on his chest, listening to the beating of his heart as he ran his hands through her hair and murmured, "I'm so sorry. You did not deserve to go through that," into her ear. She waited for the tears to come, but they didn't. She accepted what her father had done to them; she was so detached from it that when she told Arjun what happened, it felt like she was narrating something that happened to someone else. The only thing that pained her was how Arjun was processing this information. She did not doubt that this was the right thing to do. She wrapped her arms around Arjun's torso, wishing she could do something to comfort him. Do something to make this easier.

After what seemed like an eternity, Arjun pulled away.

"You're going to have to promise me two things," he began.

"Did you rehearse when we were hugging?" Pooja smiled.

"Yes, but will you promise me?"

"What do you want me to promise?"

"Firstly, I want you to come clean to Mahi once we get back. Since she is the adult you trust the most, my advice is to speak to her. You need to heal yourself completely. If you can't open up to a therapist, you can open up to her. I'm sure there is a reason she went to therapy as well. Find out, and she will help."

"Alright, I will do it once we come back from Prajwal's."

"Secondly," he cupped her face and tilted her head, looking straight into her eyes. "No more pretending. At least not with me, Avi, and Meher. We won't leave you no matter how screwed you are. Personally, I think you are beautiful, even with all the trauma you have been through. I want to see the real you. I want to be affiliated with the real you. I want to see how the trauma shaped you, what person you are because of what you went through. Also…" he hesitated. "I want to love the person you are, truly and wholeheartedly. I don't want any pretending between both of us, okay?"

"You love me?" Pooja was taken aback.

"Of course I do! You're my best friend, Pooja," Arjun smiled.

She put the sketchbook inside her bag and slung it around her shoulder, eyes burning in disappointment. Getting friend-zoned sucked, but could she blame him? He knew her for only three months. Arjun grabbed the trunk filled with books, weapons, and souvenirs that would remind her of this place. She gave her room one last sweep before she stepped outside.

Vaishnavi, Ramesh, Indra, and Avi were already waiting outside, straddling their horses. Shadow whined in delight as Pooja approached, smiling at his excitement. Vaishnavi fussed about Pooja, asking her if she packed everything, double-checking and triple-checking all the items. Ramesh stood behind her and rolled his eyes when he caught Pooja's eye.

"I'll give you three a second," Arjun said, taking Pooja's bag with him and loading it onto Shadow with Avi's help.

"Well, kiddo. Go banish some evil souls," Ramesh clapped her on the shoulder.

"Will do. I will make you proud, just wait," she smiled.

"You have already made us proud," Ramesh smiled at her.

Pooja's heart expanded.

"You take care, okay? Don't get killed. Text me even after you move into the Base. Tell me if you are safe or not after the mission. I will be worrying about you, so don't forget. Also, keep calm and focus. You can do it. Drink lots of water; it will keep you hydrated," Vaishnavi rambled.

Ramesh put a hand around his wife's shoulder. "I think she knows that, Vaishu."

"I know, it's just I'm going to miss you. Don't forget us."

"Are you kidding? You guys are literally the best. I can never forget you. I will come to visit you whenever I can. Or you can visit me. Or just come live in the Base. Ramesh can teach again. You can complete your psychology course and teach as well."

"We will consider your invitation," Ramesh smiled.

"Take care when I'm gone. I love you both," Pooja hugged Ramesh and Vaishnavi, who stiffened. Ramesh was the first to unfreeze and hug her back. Vaishnavi joined in, sobbing quietly as she squeezed the life out of Pooja.

"Can't breathe," she choked. Vaishnavi immediately released her. "Bye, guys," she waved as she walked toward Shadow.

Indra winked at her as she climbed onto him, and the four of them rode away into the forest, heading toward Prajwal's hideout.

GATECRASHING FUNERALS IS NEVER FUN

As always, the journey was the most boring, exhausting thing. They rode eastwards until midday when they had their lunches, prepared, and packed by Vaishnavi. Pooja didn't know when she got the time to do so much. They had tasty aloo parathas with achar, one of Pooja's favorite dishes. Nobody spoke much as they ate, all of them thinking about the same thing - Prajwal. After having lunch, Indra pulled out four sleeping bags and laid them on the ground.

"We have to rest. For the rest of our journey, we travel at night. This is a secret mission. Nobody knows you guys are here, as it should be. Prajwal knows you are coming after him following your speech at your pre-coronation, but he may have let his guard down as we didn't make a move for six months."

"That actually makes so much sense. Not only did the six-month time period give us time to train Pooja but also enough time for Prajwal to let down his guard," Avi commented.

"That was exactly my thinking process," Indra nodded.

"There is also the fact that people think we went on a hunting trip," Arjun added. "They don't know we met Pooja, but they will eventually, right?"

"Of course they will."

"Your plan is so great. How long did it take to make it? Five minutes?" Pooja asked.

"Are you saying there is a flaw in our plan?" Indra's voice was accusing.

"Not at all. I am just marvelling at how accurate a quote I heard is."

"What quote?" Avi inquired.

"Well, it's something about how the simplest plans turn out to be the most effective ones. Take this one, if this weren't real life, you would think the plan wasn't well-thought out. You might even think it is cliché and will fail. Doing the unexpected to fool your opponents usually is to do something so simple your opponent will be confused. They will be wondering what your big move is while you defeat them with your simpler moves."

"Sounds like something a person who plays chess would say," Arjun frowned slightly. "Do you play chess?"

"No, but my father and grandfather did before he passed away."

"Oh, I'm so sorry," Indra muttered.

"I'm not. Back then, it used to be both my grandfather and father."

"What did they used to do?" Avi asked.

"Be unsupportive," Pooja replied quickly. "You saw my dad, didn't you? My grandfather was like him."

"You have such a great family," Avi smiled and shook his head in disbelief.

"Maybe my biological family sucks, but the family I made for myself is great. You, Arjun, Indra, Ramesh, Vaishu, Meher, Mahi, there are so many good people in my life now."

"Aw, you're so cute it's making me sleepy," Avi yawned and curled up into a sleeping bag and promptly passed out.

"He can do that?" Pooja wondered.

"Yeah, him and my dad both," Arjun laughed.

"Lucky. Guess he won't be keeping watch then."

"Keeping watch?" Indra frowned. "Why?"

"When Ramesh and I were going to his house, he always kept watch, so I assumed the woods were dangerous."

"They are not. I believe Ramesh did it only because of his trauma."

"What exactly happened?"

"That's not my story to tell. Even I know only bits and pieces of it. He will tell you when he feels like it's the right time. You both go to bed," Indra lay down next to his son and fell asleep.

"Your grandfather used to hit you guys?" Arjun traced a circle on the back of Pooja's hand.

"No, but he used to yell a lot and throw things around. Plates of food, my books, anything close to him when he was raging. He was a bad father to my father who was a bad father to me. I wonder sometimes if it's genes or something and my children will suffer as well," Pooja admitted.

"No, they won't," Arjun placed his palm over her hand. "You will make a good mother, not that you have to worry about that now." Pooja laughed.

"You have something your father and grandfather didn't have – the courage to stand up for yourself. I see the determination burning in your eyes. You can change things, not only in your family but even around the world."

"You give the best pep talks," she smiled as she leaned closer to him.

"It's easy, I'm just spouting facts."

Pooja rested her head against his shoulder and closed her eyes. "You are the best," she said.

Arjun kissed the top of her head and hugged her closer to him before resting his head against the tree he was leaning on and closed his eyes. Pooja closed hers as well and fell fast asleep.

"I rolled out sleeping bags for a reason, you know," a voice jerked Pooja out from her sleep. She sat up straight, noticing Indra rolling up his sleeping bag and blushed.

"We were talking and then we fell asleep," Arjun mumbled from next to her, rubbing his eyes. "The forest just hits different in the night."

It was true. The moonlight fell on the forest floor, the mystical flowers twinkling underneath the light. The trees were quiet in a pleasant way, looking muted in the darkness. It was a scenic view, breathtaking enough to push all the thoughts of what she had to do aside, even though it was only for a short period of time.

"We have to get going, I suppose we will reach our stop soon," Indra informed as he tucked the last of his sleeping bag into his trunk tied to his horse, which was tied with the rest of them on a tree next to where they were resting.

"So soon? It's crazy how close Prajwal stays," Pooja commented as she pulled herself up.

"I keep forgetting about your ignorance," Avi nonchalantly shrugged. "You don't even know the plan."

"Of course I do," Pooja countered, "I have to go and suck the Evil Prajwal's soul out of the Good Prajwal."

"Oh yeah, piece of cake," Avi sarcastically replied.

"Life would be peaceful if you both stopped bickering," Indra rubbed his temple.

"But then, life would be boring," Avi flashed a smile.

"Whatever. Pooja, Sharanya is going to be waiting for us. Avi and I will leave you and Arjun with her. Together, you three will reach Prajwal's hideout in approximately a day's time. When you reach, after seeing Sharanya with you both, understandably, Prajwal would be in a confused state of mind. This is when you swoop in and perform the exorcism. After that, you guys can get out of there."

Pooja frowned as she sensed the obvious flaw in the plan, "When Mahi, Ahan, Avi, Arjun, and I found Sharanya, she had run away from the hideout. Prajwal's guards found her, they fought, and she escaped battered and bruised. Prajwal would know his wife is a traitor and would shoot us down as soon as we arrive."

Indra laughed, "Actually, Sharanya ensured that all the guards who saw her sneak out were killed. As far as Prajwal knows, Sharanya is pregnant and missing, presumably dead. When he sees her, he will be experiencing a lot of positive emotions, which will make the soul of Good Prajwal stronger, making it easier for you to finish your task."

"How do you know that for sure?"

"I don't, it's just a theory."

"My life depends on a theory, that's great," Pooja helped Indra untie the horses and climbed onto her own. "Wait, Ramesh told me we were going to the Base."

"Well, he doesn't know everything."

"You don't trust him?"

"It's not about trust. It's just not safe."

Pooja blinked.

Avi chuckled, interrupting their conversation, "When you die, can I read your diary?"

"My what?" Pooja turned to him, almost snapping her neck in the process.

"Oh, yeah," Arjun grinned sheepishly. "This was supposed to be a surprise, but-" He cleared his throat. "We went to your house, the one you grew up in, and retrieved all your belongings. We assumed you would, actually, we want you to stay at the Base. We prepared a room for you at the main building, and everything. I personally took up the responsibility of decorating. While I was doing that with Avi's help, we may or may not have stumbled upon your diaries."

Pooja blinked. "I don't know whether I should feel warm and fuzzy because of the room at the Base away from toxic household thing or smack you both."

"I will always be there for you when you are in doubt. For instance, right now, you should go with the warm and fuzzy feeling and hug us," Avi spread out his hands.

Pooja smacked him in the gut, just hard enough to take his breath away and mounted her horse. She straddled him as Avi stumbled to his own.

"You hit hard," he groaned. "Like, really hard."

"Must be the training," she replied. She saw Indra observing the two of them quarreling. He met her eyes and smiled, "Well, we better get going before your training kills my son."

"Nice to see you trust him so much," Pooja replied, smiling back. She knew Indra was thinking about something else and was curious to know what. She fell in step behind Indra and Arjun with Avi behind her. They followed him through the forest, taking many twists and turns which she couldn't keep track of.

In about an hour's time, Indra slowed his pace. "We are almost here," he informed.

They heard laughter, bright and loud from afar. They followed the sound. Upon reaching, the first thing Pooja noticed was the crackling fire. Sitting around it was a very visibly pregnant Sharanya, Mahi, and Ahan. She grinned and practically jumped off the horse as she ran toward them.

"Look who's ready and battle-trained," Ahan grinned wider, pulling her into a one-armed hug. Mahi joined in.

"Hey," Pooja disentangled a hand and shook Sharanya's. "What are you both doing here?" she asked Ahan and Mahi.

"We weren't going to send you off without a proper goodbye," Ahan's smile dropped. "Especially if it's the last time we might see you. If you fail, the world might just go to hell."

Pooja's smile was wiped off her face. "But no pressure?"

Mahi chuckled, "No pressure. But don't you dare mess up." She bumped her shoulder lightly. "And we can't let Sharanya travel alone; she looks like she might give birth any minute. Which is good, if Prajwal becomes normal again, everything will be superb." She smiled widely and stepped back to greet the rest of the party.

Ahan looked as if he had swallowed something extremely sour as he glared at a specific point on the ground.

"You good, bro?" Pooja mumbled as she came closer.

"Yeah, why wouldn't I be? The world could be saved today itself. How could anybody not be okay after knowing this?" He tried to smile, but it looked forced and sad.

"You know, you can have feelings about this, right? Your opinion and view do matter."

"It's the same thing."

"What?"

"Opinion and view. Same thing."

"Doesn't matter. Give me an English lecture later, for now, just tell me, what's wrong?"

"It's Prajwal not being evil," he ran a hand through his hair, forehead scrunched, "the only reason Mahi broke up with him was because he turned evil. If he turns good, what's the guarantee that she won't leave me for him? He was always better to her than me. He can give her more. I am nothing compared to him. I was always the spare."

"Is that what you think?"

"I mean, yeah."

"Bro, could you not accommodate a brain in the five-foot-nine inches of your height?" She tapped his head.

"I am six feet, and yes, I can." He pushed her hand away.

"Five nine."

"Six."

"Five nine," she said seriously.

"Bro, I am at least two inches taller than you," he rolled his eyes.

"I know. I am five seven. That makes you five nine."

"No."

"That's not the point. The point is that she won't. She started a family with you, she loves you, she will never leave you."

"Prajwal is six-three," he muttered.

"Are you not hearing what I'm saying?"

"What if Laila is just holding her back? What if she wants him but can't leave because of Laila? What if every time I touch her, she wishes it was him?" Ahan's eyes widened. "Forget I said that."

"Is that what you think?" Pooja's heart ached for him. She knew what he was feeling, if not exactly. The thought that she wasn't enough haunted her throughout her life.

"How can I not? He's everything I'm not."

"Yeah, a psychopath with too great an ambition who cares more about himself than anyone. Who, by the way, is going to be the father of twins soon."

"I don't know," Ahan smiled suddenly, and Pooja turned to see Mahi walking toward them.

"What are you two talking about?" Mahi looped her arm around Ahan.

"Relationship problems," Pooja answered honestly, but wished she had not when Mahi smiled sneakily.

"Arjun, huh? Yeah, he's the broody type, isn't he? It's okay, he's smitten. Pretty obvious, he can't take his eyes off you."

"Arjun?" Ahan frowned at Pooja. "You are too young to be vested in these kinds of things."

"Don't listen to him. Go for it."

"Maybe if I don't die today," Pooja rolled her eyes.

"Bet. If you don't die today, you ask Arjun out," Mahi quickly intervened.

"Stop rushing this for drama," she snapped.

"Well, this woman needs her fair share of it," she winked.

"Don't worry, that department is covered," Pooja flashed her a smile before gathering around Indra as he gestured for everyone to get closer.

"There's nothing more to say. Sharanya will guide you two to Prajwal's house. Technically, her house as well. Pooja, you can manipulate shadows, right?"

She nodded. It took her very little time to master shadow control, which was another cool aspect of her powers.

"You will cloak yourself and uncloak only when you see Prajwal. Then, when he is momentarily stunned, you will destroy the soul and return."

"Easy-peasy. After coming back, let's watch a movie or something," Avi added.

They all stared at him.

"Or not."

"Alright, good luck to you all. Be safe." Indra hugged Arjun, and then Pooja. He shook hands briefly with Sharanya and stepped back. Avi squished Pooja and Arjun.

"Don't die, it will be boring without you two."

"It's alright, we will haunt you," Pooja hugged him back with the same ferocity. "I'm taller than you, by the way."

Avi stepped back in mock offense and grinned. Ahan and Mahi were quick to say their goodbyes.

After the party had left, Pooja turned to Sharanya.

"So, you will be saving my husband's life?" Sharanya took her in. "The training you have is showing. You no longer look like you will pass out any second."

"Thanks, I guess," Pooja frowned. "I have a question that has been nagging me. It might be important to save Prajwal."

"Ask away," she gestured.

"How does Prajwal have the power to control humans? As far as I know, no god really specializes in that."

Sharanya paled. "Of all the questions you could ask, you asked the one most difficult to answer."

"You know me, I'm nothing but abnormal and difficult," Pooja grinned.

"True," she agreed. "Prajwal was always an ambitious man, even without being possessed. That's one quality he shares with Borkar the First. He wanted to be the best at everything. He was blessed by Lord Ganesh. Although people think it's all about knowledge, it's more about training your brain to expand and contain various information. To adapt to certain situations. If you pursue more in Ganesh's area, you start gaining immense control over your mind. Prajwal figured out how to control others' minds too. They say that the eyes are the window to the soul, right? That's true. Looking into your eyes, Prajwal can force his power into your head and mess with it. He's really powerful and dangerous."

Pooja gaped at her as she mounted her horse with little to no difficulty and began riding. Trying to calm her nerves, Pooja mounted her horse and set off behind Sharanya.

They rode, Pooja singing songs to calm herself down. Arjun slowed the pace of his horse, and Pooja followed suit.

"You don't like 'Night Changes'?" she frowned.

"Are you kidding? I absolutely love it. I had my One Direction obsession phase not too long ago."

"What?" Pooja stared incredulously.

"Yeah," he grinned, a small dimple forming on his face. "I'm pretty sure I have the posters stashed somewhere."

"Posters? Excuse me? You are more feminine than I thought."

"That's the politest way I've been called homosexual."

"Homosexual? Wow, you are fancy,"

"I am a prince."

"Humble, too."

"This is nice, right?"

"What is?"

"This," he gestured in front, as if to say everything.

"Riding to our certain deaths? You need help."

"No," he smiled again. "Just spending time alone. Talking. Making jokes."

"It's like you never had a friend."

"Most of them don't want to stop at just friends. Most of them are there for the popularity."

'I don't want to stop at friends either,' she thought. "Must be tough."

"What about you?"

"I mean, yeah, there were people who didn't want to stop at just being friends. But I wasn't very popular. I did my own thing, and people did theirs. I was close with Anu and Thals, and that's about it. It was fun. Having friends is just great," she smiled as the memories flashed through her head.

"I'm sorry, it must be difficult here."

"Not really. I mean, I do miss them a lot. But I made new friends and I wouldn't give that up for anything." She hesitated, then decided they were going to die soon anyway, so she might as well add, "I wouldn't give up meeting you for anything."

Heat flared on her face, and she glanced at Arjun, who looked equally flustered. He stared at her in complete shock, then his face lit up with a smile. He tilted his head to the side and grinned wider. He opened his mouth to say something, but before he could, Sharanya called out.

"If you both are done, we need to tether our horses here. The rest of our journey can be made on foot."

"On foot? Is that recommended for you?" Pooja glanced at her humongous belly.

Sharanya slid off her horse gracefully. She looked her in the eye, "For me, yeah. For anybody else, not really."

Pooja stared at her. Sharanya's eyes shone with a fire she recognized as hope. She stood tall, almost five foot ten in height. She had slight muscles and a toned body. Her lips were pursed, and her eyebrow raised in challenge. Her shoulder-length hair blew against her face in the slight wind, her bindi completing her really pretty, really pregnant, and really dangerous vibe.

"If you say so," she dismounted her horse with a flip and landed on her two feet next to Sharanya.

"Show-off," Sharanya muttered, chuckling, as Arjun made his way toward them.

"Should I cloak you now?"

"Yeah," Sharanya slipped her hand into Pooja's.

"Not necessary," she drew back and spread out her hands. She felt the shadows present around them and called them toward her. The abundance of darkness and the moonlight gave her a lot to work with. As she felt the power circulate through her, she took control of the shadows, bending them to hide the group.

"I can't see myself," Arjun whispered.

"That's the point, make it soundproof as well," Sharnaya said.

"What do you mean?" Pooja frowned.

"Create a barrier that does not allow sound to pass."

"Like tinted glass?"

"Yes."

"I've never done that before."

"No time like the present to try it."

Pooja focused on the swirling shadows, commanding them to do what she envisioned within her head, hoping that it would work.

"Just in case, we all stay really quiet, okay?"

Sharanya poked the swirling shadows, "Yeah, it did not work. I can hear the wind whistling."

"I can see you," Pooja gasped.

"Of course you can, only you can see us," Sharanya rolled her eyes.

"Ok, let's be quiet and go, I really don't want Pooja to exert herself," Arjun drew out a sword from his belt.

Sharanya crept forward, both of them following softly, not making any noise. Pooja's training kicked in as she became hyper-aware of the things around her. Every soft whisper of the wind, the songs the trees sang in the slight breeze, the twigs on the forest ground, the slight shiver of nervousness passing through the group, everything.

They walked at an acceptable pace until they reached a seemingly dead end, clustered with trees. Sharanya walked through them with the kids following in pursuit. They walked through the trees with a lot of grumbling to emerge at the apparent end of the forest. There was a huge wall made of black and white bricks with a tall, pitch-black tower towering over them.

"It looks like a palace for ghosts," Arjun shuddered.

"It is," Pooja exhaled.

"If you both don't shut up, we will die," Sharanya snapped.

She made her way to the wall. "We need to cross this."

"No way, that's where I draw the line. You are not climbing a wall when you are nine months pregnant," Pooja frowned.

"You're making it sound tough," she casually pressed a section of the wall, which parted open.

"Just like Harry Potter," she breathed in awe.

"What?" Sharanya frowned.

"You know, going to Diagon Alley through the Leaky Cauldron."

"What is Harry Potter?" Sharanya frowned. "This was my genius design."

"'What is Harry Potter?'" Pooja looked around. "Are you kidding me?"

"Let's go," Arjun linked his arm around her bicep and led her through the hole in the wall. As soon as Sharanya pressed another section, it closed up.

She frowned. "Why is this place so empty?"

She was right. The palace was located an easy hundred meters away from where they were standing, and there wasn't a single soul in sight.

"Maybe Prajwal thought that nobody would come from here?"

"Hopefully," Sharanya frowned and touched her belly, "but keep up the shadows just in case."

Pooja nodded and studied the swirling shadows. "You guys can see, right?"

"Obviously," Sharanya and Arjun rolled their eyes. Pooja flushed, and they kept moving at a slow pace.

They walked the whole back end of the palace, not encountering a single being, and spread into a courtyard which was bustling with tons of people dressed in white. At the far end was a small stage with a huge photo frame placed on a stool with garlands around it. Next to it stood Prajwal, flanked by a guy Pooja had never seen.

He was dressed in a simple white dhoti and an *angavastram*. The dhoti came up to his knees, showing off his strong legs. The *angavastram* covered little to none of his torso, which was gleaming with scars and a thin layer of sweat. His abs and muscles were well-defined and bulging, causing most of the crowd to ogle at him. His face was bent to the ground, exposing only the neat dark hair covering his head.

A priest stood on the opposite side of the photo, chanting in Sanskrit and sprinkling holy water onto the picture. He stepped back and bowed to Prajwal.

Prajwal stepped forward, and Pooja finally got a good look at him. He had a lean build, not too skinny but not muscular either. His torso was sliced with numerous scars, some of them looked fresh. His hair was shabby, the curls messed up and cut short. His cocky grin was replaced by an emotionless expression. His eyes looked hollow and defeated. He looked like he might collapse at any moment.

"Thank you, great priest, for performing the last rites of my wife," Prajwal announced. To his credit, his voice did not even tremble. "I would like to express my gratitude with this donation."

The muscular guy next to him moved forward, a plate in hand filled with rice, clothes, money, and fruits which he had obtained from a nearby servant. The priest accepted the donation gracefully and exited the stage, leaving a weary Prajwal and the tense muscular guy on stage.

"Thank you, everyone, for attending this occasion today. My wife was my everything, along with that, she was also a mother to each one of you." At this, the muscular guy tensed more, looking up at the crowd.

Pooja gasped.

His face was a mirror image of her father's, with the same hard-set jaw and lines marking the high cheekbones and sharp jawline. His eyes, however, were emerald green, twinkling in the lamplight, filled with unshed tears.

"We have honored her today, we have spent the last few months searching for her, for your mother, but to no avail. There is one thing I have not had the heart to share with you all until today. My wife was carrying my child when she was kidnapped. She and my unborn child were killed by those power-hungry so-called dharmic warriors. For the sins they have committed against us, we will attack them. We have the Prince and the Princess with us. We are undefeatable, we will destroy the devas and emerge victorious!"

The crowd erupted into cheers and stomped on the ground, sending tremors.

"Now," Sharanya nudged Pooja, who immediately removed the cloak shielding her.

"Prajwal!" she cried.

Time seemed to slow down as Prajwal registered Sharanya. His eyes widened in shock, then pure happiness. Tears began to flow from his eyes as he rushed forward, crossing the courtyard within seconds. He stopped in front of Sharanya, reaching out but not touching her.

"Sharanya," he whispered as if that one word meant the world to him. "Sharanya."

"Prajwal," she sobbed as she pulled him close.

He touched their foreheads together. "What..."

"Shh," she hushed, wrapping her arms around him. He let his head fall onto her shoulder and shook with his sobs.

Pooja blinked back the tears she didn't realize had formed in her eyes. She took a deep breath and focused on Prajwal. She felt two souls beating in sync, one soul shining bright. It felt positive, so she focused on the other one. She knew immediately that it was the Evil Prajwal. The soul itself seemed to emit darkness and spite, so she extended her hand, willing her power to wrap itself around the soul.

A hush had fallen over the crowd, though Pooja barely noticed it. She forced the grip to tighten, and she pulled hard.

"What? Sharanya, what?" Prajwal's desperate cries sounded through the courtyard. Pooja opened her eyes and saw Sharanya struggling to keep a grip on her husband.

She closed her eyes and focused with all her will. She pulled the soul out of Prajwal's mouth and snapped her eyes open. She saw the mass of darkness hovering in front of her. Prajwal slumped in Sharanya's arms.

"Pooja," the soul whispered, sending chills down her spine.

Her name, coming from the creature in front of her, possessed by the hate and rage, engulfed her in fear. Her eyes widened as she took in what she was facing, for the first time understanding the gravity of the situation. Prajwal was one of the most powerful Ganesh's to exist, and he himself was not able to fight the spirit. What chance did Pooja have?A gentle voice whispered in the back of her head, "Fear is your strongest enemy, succumb to it and you have already lost." The numbness vanished slowly, the soothing voice leaving behind a calming effect. She remembered Ramesh's advice, "When you feel scared, you have to defuse the situation. Your opponent wants to be in power. Show them that you are unaffected by them, which will instantly put you on the same level as them. Use your humor to hurt them, to dethrone them. Use your words."

"Prajwal Borkar," Pooja sneered, rolling her eyes. "Look, I *finally* meet the living legend. Or should I say dead? The past few decades haven't treated you well, I see."

"You have no idea," the spirit mused. "But I will be much better after crushing you and your little companions."

"Oh, I'm terrified," Pooja replied, fighting the fear that was crawling into her head once again.

The spirit seemed to stretch itself, growing into a dark mass, the shape of a human. Within minutes, before her stood the shell of the human Prajwal was. A dark humanoid shape with two whites for eyes that glowed red in hatred. The reek of evil wafted through the air, assaulting her nose.

"You should be. Your kind has slowly destroyed humanity without fearing repercussions," he seemed to smile. "Did you really think there wasn't going to be consequences?"

"Consequences?" Pooja's head felt weird, as if someone was poking her head with sharp spears. "What do you mean?"

"So, you're telling the Base is vulnerable and it doesn't trust its sacrificial lambs?" The spirit actually laughed.

"Sacrificial lamb?" Pooja's head was throbbing insistently now, not letting her focus. The world seemed to blur a little.

"You can't defeat me because good wins over evil. You've joined the wrong side," the spirit curled its fingers, and Pooja felt herself stepping toward him. The spirit glided toward her, slowly, as if he had all the time in the world. "Your gods have crushed asuras for no reason. You have never given us any rights and treated all of us like vermin. Our emperor Bali, a demon, worshipped the gods and what did he get? He lost his life and entire dynasty. That's the gods' justice!"

Pooja nodded; it made sense. The gods never cared about the Blessed either, never communicating with them. The asuras, however, were just misunderstood and brutalized by humans and gods.

"Yes," the spirit hissed as if he could read her mind. "They killed some of the greatest kings in the world and twisted the stories after they cheated. In the end, the one who wins writes history."

"You're right," Pooja mumbled, feeling her brain slowly shutting out the rest of the world. She frowned; something felt very wrong. The feeling was instantly eased. From the corner of her eye, she could see Sharanya and Arjun holding Prajwal, looking at her with utter fear in their eyes. Sharanya was tearing up, clutching her unconscious husband to her chest, looking at her pleadingly.

"Look at me," the spirit hissed, and Pooja turned her head. "You're my descendant too. Prajwal was a weak vessel, but I sense immense power in you. Let me in, let us share your mortal body. Together, we can eradicate evil from this world."

"You want to possess me?" Pooja muttered sleepily. Yes, something was off.

"No," the spirit softly caressed her face. "I want us to work together, I want to help you. If you let me, there will be no more caste systems, no more poverty, the asuras will make the world a better place."

The promises echoed in her mind, and she couldn't remember why the spirit in front of her was evil. She felt a presence in her mind, sorting through her memories until it found the one of her father. He beat her up, threw her bloodied into her room, and refused to let her out for three days. She was nearly hospitalized after that.

"First," the spirit purred, "We will get rid of this monster. Let's torture him like he ruined you."

Pooja wanted that so badly. The solution to all her problems would be to kill that monster. It would be a mercy to the people around him.

"How does he know about that?" the gentle voice that calmed her asked.

It hit her like a slap; the spirit was in her head, twisting her thoughts. She found the presence instantly, rammed into it, forcing it out, out, out. Pooja fell to the floor, gasping as the numbness disappeared and feeling hit her with great might. The spirit towered over her, disappointment coming off of him in waves.

"Well, if you won't join me, I will destroy you," he simply raised his hand, preparing to strike. Pooja was utterly defenceless. She was exhausted and drained of her reserves. Pooja was going to die and she couldn't stop it. Suddenly, he was surrounded by water. It flowed around him, encompassing him, trapping him inside. The water kept flowing, lifting him off the ground, showing the man who looked like her father standing. With his *dhoti, angavastram,* and hair gently flowing behind him, and the terrible anger in his eyes, he looked like a god letting out his wrath. He moved the cocoon with a small jerk of his head, displaying his immense power.

His emerald eyes met Pooja's, assessing her. "Do it," he said. That's all he said before turning his attention back to Pooja's trapped ancestor. She rose shakily to her feet, taking the support of Simba, who had appeared without anybody noticing.

Pooja tried to summon any form of energy, but found none pulsing through her veins. Sweat beaded on her saviour's forehead; he was going to lose control of the water soon. Hopelessness crashed into her.

"Put your hand on me," Simba ordered, "palm outstretched."

Pooja obeyed and felt tendrils of power snaking up her palm from Simba. She looked up at him and saw determination in her guide's eyes.

"It will kill you," Pooja sighed, trying to talk him out of it.

"My life is tied to yours," he simply said, closing his eyes.

Pooja took a shuddering breath, absorbing all the magic. She opened her eyes just as the water cocoon collapsed. Her magic flew out of her like a whip, surrounding itself around the spirit, locking itself onto every evil tendril of the spirit. Pooja wrapped her grip tighter around the soul, forcing it into a ball. She kept tightening and compressing it until there was a huge ball of energy in the centre. She took control of each atom of the soul by covering it with her power, as if it were muscle memory, and exploded it.

The explosion shook the place, blasting Pooja backward. She flew high before her head slammed against the walls of the palace, and she slid down. The world went dark.

FAMILY REUNIONS ARE ALWAYS WEIRD

Pooja woke up on a horse that was galloping as if its life depended on it. After all that she had seen, she assumed it did.

"Faster," a deep voice groaned behind her.

She suddenly realized that muscular arms were wrapped around her waist, holding her steady on the horse. She was leaning against someone extremely rigid and strong. She looked up to see the muscular dude standing next to Prajwal, staring straight ahead, and realized she was in his arms.

She tried to wriggle free from his grip when he looked down at her with a stern expression.

"Stop moving, I'm saving you, you idiot," he hissed. "We don't have time for this, can't you be unconscious for some more time?"

"Don't talk to her like that," Arjun's angry voice came from their left before he arrived on his horse, keeping pace with theirs. "How are you?" he asked her.

Pooja felt as if her insides were being microwaved. Her throat was drier than the Sahara desert, she had a massive headache, and had barely any control over her limbs. She was pretty sure she looked like she had gone through hell and come back. She nodded a universal "I'm fine" gesture. Arjun did not seem convinced.

The muscular guy whipped the horse, which Pooja recognized as Shadow, encouraging it to move faster. Where was Simba?

"Hey!" Pooja protested, her throat raspy as hell.

"Whoa," the guy chuckled, "You sound dead."

Pooja rolled her eyes, resigning herself to the fact that she had to deal with this guy for longer.

"Your boyfriend wanted to ride with you, but the only horse that would let me ride it was Shadow. Shadow lets only two people ride him so far: me and you."

Pooja wanted to ask why. She also wanted to know his name and why they were riding with him. She also wanted to know the condition of her guide; however, as she seemed to have lost the ability to speak, she closed her eyes, leaned back, and fell asleep.

She woke up once she felt them slow down, slid off the horse ungracefully, and fell face-first onto the forest floor. She heard the thump of boots and a snicker before she was pulled to her feet by the muscular guy. She heard Sharanya and Prajwal's horse approaching before she saw the two dismount. Arjun came in last, his hair ruffled but otherwise perfect, looking at her in worry.

He frowned at the muscular guy holding her.

"You are squeezing her biceps too tightly, Krishna. You will hurt her," he said.

'Who the hell is Krishna?' Pooja wondered.

"It's fine, your little girlfriend is safe," the muscular guy - Krishna - laughed before twirling her around and catching her in a dip. "See, a graceful dancer she is too," he noted as Pooja struggled to balance herself.

Arjun took her from his arms gently and scowled at Krishna. He set her down, back to the tree, and gave her a flask of water as Prajwal and Krishna tied the horses.

Pooja gulped down the water, immediately feeling better.

"Where..." she began.

"Not now, Sharanya's water broke. She's going to give birth any second now," Arjun turned away and began getting things out of Sharanya's pack. Krishna and Prajwal set up the tent as Sharanya sank to the ground. Arjun removed an inflatable mattress, gloves, and other medical items that Pooja didn't know the names of. He shoved them all inside the tent as Prajwal carried Sharanya inside.

Arjun came out, ashen-faced. "Will you be okay?"

"Yeah," Pooja replied, mortified.

"Okay, wish me luck. I'm going to go deliver a baby in the middle of nowhere."

"Babies," Pooja corrected.

"Oh, joy," he replied, giving her a nervous smile and re-entering the tent.

'Simba!' Pooja called out.

'Pooja,' Simba's weak voice answered.

'You're okay,' Pooja whispered, tears finally sliding down her face as she rested the back of her head on the trunk of the tree.

'It'll take more than that to kill the two of us,' Simba reassured, his voice strained.

'You should rest,' she told him.

'I'm fine,' Simba tried to sound stronger but failed.

'Please,' Pooja begged. Her head went silent, indicating that her guide had actually listened to her.

Pooja then heard Sharanya's groans that turned into whimpers, then screams from the tent. She bit on her knuckles as the screams grew louder, more painful, and more desperate.

"Please! God!" Sharanya's screams echoed in the forest. Pooja dismissed the urge to hurl or sob. Her imagination took over, getting darker with the screams. After what felt like forever, the tent quietened only for the sounds of a baby's cry to emit from it. She heard whoops of joy from the guys inside.

"That's baby one. Let's move to the other one," came Sharanya's weak voice.

The screams were heard for a comparatively shorter amount of time before the cries of another baby sounded.

"Congratulations, Mr and Mrs Borkar, you are now parents to two beautiful baby boys," Krishna announced.

Arjun staggered out of the tent, his face gleaming with sweat. He took off his surgical mask and gloves. Shaking uncontrollably, he sat next to Pooja.

"You did great," she grinned at him.

He shook his head, still trembling, and fell onto her shoulder, burying his face in her hair. She held him tight until the shaking subsided.

"Who gave birth, you or Sharanya?" Krishna joked. Arjun jumped back and onto his feet. He glared at Krishna, who seemed unperturbed about the experience. "Want to see the baby?" he asked Pooja, who nodded.

He grabbed her by the waist and shooed her into the room, Arjun trailing behind. She saw Prajwal and Sharanya cradling a baby each, looking at each other with smiles that could illuminate the darkest of places. Sharanya said something to which Prajwal threw his head back and laughed. Watching him laugh, she smiled.

"I missed you," she said softly, laying the baby on her lap and cupping his face.

Prajwal leaned into her palm. "I did too. I thought you were dead; you are everything to me. I hope…"

"Later," she sighed.

"Later," he agreed before leaning forward and kissing her softly.

"Guys, ew," Krishna interrupted.

Prajwal disentangled himself from his wife to mockingly glare at her when he noticed Pooja. His smile dropped as he stared at her with discomfort.

"Thank you for everything."

She nodded, unsure of what to do. She walked up to him tentatively and peered at the baby.

"Do you want to hold him?" he asked.

"Yeah, but it is unhygienic," she replied.

He nodded, and the awkward silence stretched on.

"I'm sorry," he began.

"Dude, I was a baby. You gotta say sorry to Mahi and Ahan, who are waiting for us back at the base. We have to talk about a lot of things, but for now, just be happy. We will be out of your hair."

Prajwal smiled at her tentatively and turned back to his wife. Pooja grinned, feeling ridiculously happy at their happiness and ushered the boys out of the tent. They sat at a fair distance.

"That was nice of you, giving him some time to rest before springing the doubts, insults, and stuff," Krishna said.

"He deserves it. The poor man was not in control of his own body for years. I can't imagine how free he must be feeling right now."

She rested her head on Arjun's shoulder, intertwining their fingers. He put his head on hers, and they stayed there for a while, happy to be alive. They finally got up, unable to tolerate the grumbling Krishna any longer, pulled a tent out of their pack – their only tent – and unrolled their sleeping bags. It was crowded with three people, but they managed to drift into an uncomfortable sleep.

They woke early the next morning when Arjun texted his dad to pick them up in a carriage. How he got cell service in the woods was a mystery. They ate some food that they had packed and got ready to enter grandiosely into the palace.

"How did you have all the supplies to deliver the baby?" Pooja wondered aloud as she helped pack the tents, pressing a few buttons until they shrank into a simple hankie.

"We prepared for the worst by packing all the things just in case I delivered," Sharanya answered groggily. She had been drifting in and out of sleep, obviously exhausted after giving birth. Prajwal hovered around her, occasionally adjusting the blanket, getting her to drink water, wrapping the babies, and looking at them as if he had everything in the world. This was the Prajwal Borkar Mahi fell in love with, and it was easy to see why.

Which made her think about Ahan. She knew that there was no way Prajwal or Mahi would catch feelings for each other again. She had seen how they looked at their respective spouses. She just wanted to know what made Ahan so insecure in the first place, as she was sure there was more to the story than just Prajwal. To be honest, Ahan was the best person for Mahi; he was perfect for her in every way.

She shook her head; this wasn't her business. It was between Ahan, Prajwal, Mahi, and Sharanya. She shouldn't interfere. She glanced at the two boys, who seemed to be non-verbally arguing with each other. They were standing a few feet apart, glaring at each other. Actually, Arjun was the one who was glaring, while Krishna just smiled and laughed.

The resemblance Krishna had to her father had Pooja's mind reeling. The carefree and fun nature of his was a contrast from her rather harsh father. She wondered if her father was ever as joyful as Krishna in his life, and wondered what it would've been like if her father was also jovial like him now. She closed her eyes and pressed her forehead to her knees, trying to force the aching feeling in her heart away. It did not help at all.

"You good?" Krishna's hand was on her shoulder. She looked up at his emerald eyes, filled with concern.

"Yes," she said, shaking her head. "No, I'm tired, that's all." She felt bad lying to him, but it wasn't like she knew him and she wasn't going to tell a random stranger about what she was thinking. Arjun, however, could know.

"Can you excuse us, please?" she asked Krishna.

"Well, you did say please," he smiled and walked off, staring into the distance.

"What happened?" Arjun sat next to her.

She told him what she was thinking. Arjun remained silent for a long time. Too long.

"I'm sorry. I overthink a lot. I should stop dumping everything on you. I'll handle it on my own."

"That's the thing," he sighed, rumpling his hair, "You are not alone. I know that you are going through some huge thing right now, and I am so glad you opened up to me. I don't want you to stop. I want to know every single thought that you have and want to share. I want to know you in the purest form." He hesitated, "If that's okay. You can tell me if I'm going too far. But I would die to know the real you. I told you this before, you always seem to be forgetting, idiot."

Pooja could have kissed him right then and there, but she smiled and smothered him in a hug instead. He pretended to be unable to breathe.

"I can't breathe. You are strangling me."

She laughed and pulled away. He leaned forward, his breath fanning her face. She froze, feeling heat creeping up her face, her heart racing against her will, her throat drying up again. He pressed his lips against her cheek softly.

"You are not alone," he assured her softly, placing another kiss on the top of her head. She melted completely, physically forcing herself not to cry. She felt the tears overpower her will and hugged him, staying in his arms and letting the tears flow, slow and steady, lifting a great burden off her shoulders.

"Thank you," she whispered.

He didn't reply. He didn't have to.

Pooja heard the creak of a chariot and the neighing of horses. Not taking any risks, she drew out her sword, just as the rest of her party became alert. Prajwal drew out a dagger, Sharanya's dagger. Arjun knocked an arrow, and Krishna stood with a sword. The chariot came into view, with Indra sitting in his royal attire. Prajwal immediately surrendered his weapon and sank to the ground in surrender.

When Indra stepped off the carriage, he bowed low in utmost respect. Indra barely spared a glance. His eyes were fixated on Krishna, whose sword was sheathed.

"Who are you, boy?" he inquired.

"I am Krishna, Prajwal's nephew, My King," Krishna replied with a bow.

"There is no way. You are a spitting image of Jayanth," he said as he seized his shoulders. "Who are you?"

"My King," Prajwal said, "he is really the first child of Jayanth and Jyothi Bahl."

"What?" Pooja and Krishna gasped.

"Yes. Three years prior to your birth, when your mother found out she was carrying Krishna, a couple of asuras stole him from the womb," he turned to Indra. "They arranged a womb-like condition for him to grow as a zygote. After the birth, I joined them, and we raised him to be on our side. He is the prince who was on our side. After he grew older, around a few months ago, we introduced him to your daughter. They both have been in a relationship for a while now. The plan was to bring her to our side and take you guys down."

"You never told me that," Krishna snapped. "You said I'd be king, that's all, and that Aadhya would be my queen."

"I said you were destined to. I'm surprised you didn't find out," Prajwal lowered his eyes in regret.

"What? I..." Krishna broke off.

"Oh God, Aadhya? She's the Princess, and you two have been... Did you know?" Indra asked.

"No," Krishna reassured him, "I didn't know she was the Princess. Everyone did but me, apparently," he snapped, shooting a dirty look in Prajwal's direction.

Indra ran a hand across his face and began to pace.

"Krishna," Prajwal tentatively stepped toward him. "I'm so sorry, my boy."

"My whole life you've told me that my parents were dead. That Indra killed them. Now, I'm getting to know that they're alive, I have a sister, and my whole life was nothing but a lie to make me evil, just like you," he fumed.

Prajwal stepped back as if he had been slapped. Indra chose the right time to stop pacing.

"Krishna, how old are you?"

"Seventeen," he replied, the rage still smouldering in his eyes, making him look exactly like her father.

"You come of age in a year," Indra pursed his lips. "You're the Prince, there's no denying it. You look just like Jayanth before..." His voice trailed away, and his eyes met Pooja's. "We still have a year to prepare you to be King. Convincing people you're the Prince would be difficult."

"No, it won't," Krishna stated.

"Well, you have to understand," Indra began.

"No," Krishna laughed with no humour. "Once the Prince and the Princess are found, they can touch the bracelet and it will glow. According to the legends, the Prince has to wear it while ruling; apparently, it will help them rule well or something. Did you not know that?"

"No, I didn't. How did *you* know?" Indra wondered.

"I read a copy of the original text of the legend; Prajwal had one on him when he escaped the Base. I wondered why. Of course, if I were smart enough, I would've known," Krishna shot Prajwal a disgusted look.

Prajwal hung his head, chewing on his bottom lip. Pooja felt slightly bad for him, understanding how controlling and influential Borkar the First could be with first-hand experience. She wondered how much longer he would be blamed for the choices he didn't make.

Indra stared at him, speechless. There was a moment of silence, then he spoke up.

"Alright, we will announce your existence to the world when we reach, make the warrior prince who helped his sister and Arjun defeat Prajwal. This is going to be tough to explain, but I hope you can charm the crowd."

"I was trained for that, uncle."

Indra nodded at the casual tone Krishna took on. He didn't notice the battle that Pooja saw in his eyes, the look of one's life turning upside down. Indra glanced at Arjun, a worried expression flashing across his face.

"All these years you have trained for are nothing. I wish I wasn't as ignorant as I was," he softly said. He walked up to Arjun and cupped his face in his hands. Pooja was amazed at how similar they looked; Arjun was almost his father's height. Their similarities were clear as daylight in the shadows.

"I am so sorry, my boy," he said sincerely.

"It's alright, Dad," Arjun stepped closer and hugged his father, who reciprocated with equal enthusiasm.

Pooja clambered onto Shadow, refusing to go in the carriage. Sharanya, her babies, and Prajwal were let into it, followed by Krishna. The horse was added to the many drawing the carriage. Arjun politely refused to ride in the carriage, mounting his horse instead. The carriage rode forward, leaving Arjun and Pooja to follow behind.

"So," Arjun laughed, "What the hell, right?"

"Well, yeah, things are changing quickly."

"I don't know whether for the better or worse," Arjun gravely replied.

"I have a feeling for the better. A new perspective will help solve the problems you found in the Base."

"Yeah, we can. We'll make changes and hey, we might have actually stopped the war today," Arjun grinned. "Can I ask something?"

"Yes?" She drew her horse closer to his.

"About what Krishna said, about us and all," Arjun started.

Pooja cringed. "Look, I'm going to be really honest with you. I really don't want anything right now. I mean, we are just kids, there's a lot of time to decide. I want to focus on my education and career for starters. I haven't had formal education, so I'm basically illiterate according to your standards. Even though I'm fully educated with my powers, I've technically had only one week of schooling. There's so much more for me to do. I have to decide which career path I'm going to choose and, well, you get it."

"Um…" he chuckled awkwardly. "Pooja, you're a really amazing person, but, um, I don't see you like that. I really like Meher, and since you're her best friend, I thought you could help me ask her out."

"Sure," Pooja blinked. "I just didn't want to hurt your feelings, so I said all that."

"Thank God," Arjun laughed, and Pooja joined in, her heart shattering into tiny pieces.

"How did you two, you know…" Pooja gestured.

"Well," he blushed, grinning. "After you left, we sort of began working on fixing the Base thing together. We got close, had a few moments, and I realized that God, she's gorgeous. She's so smart, funny; she's literally perfect, I'm not even lying. I think there's a chance I'm going to fall in love with her!"

Pooja grinned. They got close working on something *Pooja* put them up to. Awesome! That's perfect. *Wow.*

The chariot in front stopped, and Pooja looked up, not wanting to dwell on Arjun-Meher, and saw Krishna step out. He grinned at them before climbing behind Pooja.

"What are you doing?" she asked.

"Indra agreed that leaving you two alone is not wise," he said, humour lacing his voice. Humour as a self-defence mechanism, classic. Pooja did it too, but still- *classic.*

Arjun glowered at him, "That's why you're here?"

"Is that how you speak to your future king slash brother-in-law?" Krishna inquired, laughing.

Pooja elbowed him, "Drop it. It's not like that between us."

"No, Prajwal and Indra are talking about all of Prajwal's plans and stuff, cleaning up the stuff. I'm not allowed to listen because I need to be taken care of as well."

"They're gonna kill you?" Pooja gasped.

"No, idiot. They want to shape me to be the perfect king for them," he snorted. "Good luck."

"Hey, can I ask something?" Pooja wondered.

"Sure," Krishna said.

"Why were you being weird when you first saw me?"

"I wanted to piss off Arjun."

"Why?"

"He's too Prince Charming for me to handle. Done asking questions?" he tugged her hair.

"Yeah," she stared at her brother. Her *brother*.

"I have a personal request," Krishna sighed, flicking her arm.

"What is that?" Arjun asked with malice in his voice.

"I want to meet my real parents. I thought who better to take me than you, Pooja. Indra told me to ask you about it first."

Pooja stiffened. "They aren't really the best parents in the world. Especially not my father. But you deserve your own opinion of them; just don't expect me to play nice."

"How could I? We have the same stubborn fire in us." He hugged her lightly from behind.

Pooja smiled. The whole world turned upside down; there were so many changes that needed to be implemented. The expected course of the world went haywire, but at least all hope was not lost. However, twisted the world was, at least there were people who could see the reality and try to fix it. Hope for humanity wouldn't be lost as long as someone stubborn enough steps in to eradicate the problem. Prophecy or not, the conditions they were brought up in shaped them into the people they are now. People the world desperately needs. People who become heroes to save humanity.